Unattainable

No Rival #5

Charity Parkerson

I0527891

Punk & Sissy Publications
--Warning: This book is intended for

readers over the age of 18.

Copyright © 2016 Charity Parkerson
Editor: Vicky Reese
Cover art by Dar Albert
ISBN-10:1-946099-05-8
ISBN-13:978-1-946099-05-1
Note: This book was originally published under the same title
with Ellora's Cave Publishing.

Book 5 in the No Rival series

A career-ending injury leaves Brian reeling. With no clue what he'll do now that his dream of becoming an MMA champion is over, he is shocked at an unexpected offer of help from a former champ.

Terry has seen the top and is happy with his life in retirement. However, the chance to help a fellow fighter regain his dream is something he can't resist.

When Brian accepts Terry's offer, the sexual magnetism between them catches Brian off guard. Keeping his attraction hidden becomes a bigger challenge than regaining his strength. Plus, Terry's mixed signals leave Brian frustrated and confused.

Though Terry is just as hot for Brian, he has secrets that could tear their budding romance apart. But he simply cannot resist the pull Brian has over him or the heat between them. Through it all, both men discover that love really can conquer all.

Acknowledgment

The **No Rival** series has challenged me in ways I never expected. Days of crying, laughing, blushing and talking to myself in the grocery store grew into characters I truly love. They haven't always behaved the way I planned but they've lived the life meant for them. Now, I need to thank a few people who have allowed me to be me along the way. Touching my heart shouldn't go without acknowledgment.

Vicky Reese for having the best editing comments ever. It takes amazing talent to make an author laugh while correcting their work. I hope you find chocolate you've hidden from yourself on a daily basis and it never sticks to your hips.

Romancing the Book for leaving me humbled. Being considered one of your favorite GBLT authors meant more than I can say.

Finally, for every reader who takes a chance on me. You're beautiful.

Chapter One

February 14th

He'd been sold at auction. Of course, it was ridiculous for Brian to complain. He'd volunteered, after all. No Rival, the fight club he belonged to and worked for, had hosted a private auction to raise money for a local children's hospital. Several of the fighters, himself included, were handing over eight hours of their time to the highest bidders. When he'd signed up, Brian had thought nothing of it. The proceeds were going to a good cause and he didn't mind helping out. He'd fetched a good price too, so he shouldn't complain. The problem was who'd bought him. The memory of light green eyes flashed across his mind. The muscles in his shoulders tensed. His cock twitched. Nothing good could come of this.

"It looks like you could use a lift."

Brian's gaze flickered in Terry's direction at the sound of his voice. Terry Richards wasn't especially tall, maybe only five-ten. He was a good five inches shorter than Brian was, but he was solid muscle.

Brian grunted. "Yeah. It looks that way."

"Come on then," Terry said, motioning for Brian to follow. "You did a good thing tonight. Giving McKenna and Kurt your car," he clarified as Brian fell in step beside him.

Brian held his silence. He hoped it turned out to be. His best friend, McKenna, had been his date to the auction. While he'd lost his soul to the highest bidder, her ex had shown up, obviously intent on winning her back. When he realized the pair needed some

9

time alone, he'd loaned them his car in hopes they would work things out. McKenna was pregnant. She needed Kurt. Of course now, as Brian climbed inside Terry's Chevy pickup, he worried it had been a mistake. Not for McKenna. For him.

Turning over the ignition, Terry fired up the heat. He didn't move. Brian wanted to smack himself. "Oh. I live on Grove Avenue off Fifty-Second."

Terry still didn't budge. An uncomfortable silence grew. At one time Terry had been the World Divisional MMA Middleweight Champion. It was a position Brian coveted. Unfortunately, he'd sustained a career-ending injury a few months earlier. The dream was lost to him now. The fact Terry once held the position Brian wanted for himself had nothing to do with his discomfort. Additionally, Terry being—for the most part—a stranger to him, also had nothing to do with the reason Brian was ready to jump out of the truck. It was the man's light-green gaze, combined with the knowledge he now owned Brian for one whole day of his choosing, that caused chill bumps to rise on Brian's skin. Terry kicked up the heat a notch, proving how closely he'd been watching Brian.

He wanted to say something, anything to break the silence. Brian couldn't think of a single topic. Words were lost to him.

"My offer still stands. I'd love to help you get back on track for the title."

There was that too. The day they'd met, Terry had volunteered to help Brian find his way back to the road to the championship. Brian really didn't want to train with Terry. Unfortunately, he couldn't think of a gracious way to say no. Terry had made his offer while Brian had been in the hospital. The last thing he wanted was a pity session. Instead of answering, he decided to deflect.

"You're retired. Enjoy it."

"This is my way of enjoying it," Terry countered, making Brian want to groan. It wasn't in frustration as it should've been. Nope. For him, it was sexual all the way. Brian eyed the black wool pea coat hiding Terry's delicious body from view. He hated the jacket for a moment. It was unhealthy how much he loathed an inanimate object.

"Why?" Honestly, Brian didn't care. He was simply fulfilling his end of the conversation with a mundane question. Otherwise, he might do something stupid, like admit he didn't want to train with Terry because he couldn't handle the thought of the man's body against his.

"How much did McKenna tell you about my brother?"

Brian supposed he knew quite a bit. He was equally aware there could be a thousand things he didn't know. "They were married. He was sick and killed himself." It was the cliff notes version, of course. It wasn't as if the man didn't know his brother had died. Unfortunately, Brian hadn't intended for his words to sound quite so unfeeling. Terry's sadness was almost tangible. Brian wanted to kick his own ass. "I'm sorry," he said automatically but Terry waved it away.

"I'm guessing what she didn't tell you is how I abandoned him to her care as fast as I could."

In spite of the situation, a chuckle fell from Brian's lips. When he pictured what he knew about McKenna, he couldn't imagine her feeling any such thing. Terry's brother Gray had been McKenna's whole world before he died. He flashed Terry an apologetic smile. "It seems I'll be telling you I'm sorry quite a bit tonight. It's only—well—you know McKenna." He shrugged. "She once admitted to me that Gray was who she based her devil character on in her books. Considering the hot as hell erotica she writes, I'm inclined to think you probably made a good decision by leaving his care in her capable hands."

Terry looked as if he was fighting back a smile. Brian glanced away before the hunger gnawing at his gut showed on his face. He'd hate to get kicked out to the curb on such a cold night. He was stupid, wanting a man who most likely had never looked at another guy the way Brian was looking at him.

"I was content to let her have it," Terry said, dragging Brian back on topic.

"It wasn't that I didn't love him. I simply didn't know how to help. Everyone, including me, treated him differently after his diagnosis. McKenna was the only person who didn't fail him. There isn't a day goes by that I don't wish I could have him back, do things over." Terry shrugged. "Maybe one day I'll feel like I've made amends. Until then, I'm trying to help as many people as I can. I want to make a difference."

"At the risk of sounding like an ungrateful ass, I don't have any interest in being your charity case."

A mocking grin touched his lips. "Oh. I think we both know you're different." Brian had no idea what Terry meant. "Plus," Terry added, "You don't have much choice in the matter. At least not for eight hours, anyhow. I paid a lot of money for you."

"Damn." He had. A triumphant expression crossed Terry's face at Brian's curse. "Do you still have my number?"

"Yeah," Brian admitted sounding petulant even to his ears. He crossed his arms over his chest.

"Good. Text me."

"Okay."

"Well. I'm waiting."

"Now?" Brian asked, hearing the irritation in his voice but unable to stop it.

"I believe I just said so."

Sighing heavily, Brian fished out his phone and found Terry's card in his wallet. He dialed the number, sending a quick "hello".

"There," Brian said, slipping the phone back inside his pocket. Terry's buzzed, sounding loud in the otherwise quiet car. His grin transformed into something almost sinister.

"I'll send you my address. Be there at ten a.m., no excuses."

"Not that I'm making one, but I'm not allowed to train for at least another two weeks with the damage to my thigh." A week earlier, Brian had ripped open his femoral artery making an ass out of himself with McKenna after a night of heavy drinking. Luckily, she'd known exactly what to do to keep him from bleeding out. Unfortunately, it set his training back...again.

Terry pulled away from the curb. With his eyes locked on the road, the smirk never left his face. Brian was fascinated. He couldn't look away. "For what I have planned, you won't need your leg."

His brain hiccupped. There was no other way to describe how Brian's mind blanked for a complete minute. For a moment, Terry's tone almost sounded as if he was propositioning him. Of course, it was most likely wishful thinking on his part, but still, Brian's dick didn't care. It beat against his zipper, begging to come out and play.

He cleared his throat twice. Terry's mocking grin hitched up a notch at the sound. "What if I don't have my car back by then?" Brian asked, trying a different track.

"You will." The confidence in Terry's voice made it impossible for him to argue. "Okay," Brian drawled, determined not to say another word. If his car didn't magically reappear in the middle of the night, then he wouldn't have to worry about showing up—problem solved. They made the rest of the short drive in silence while Brian did his best not to inhale Terry's scent. It was impossible, of course.

He smelled amazing. As Terry turned onto Grove Avenue, Brian pointed out a small cluster of apartments.

"I'm right there in Building C." Since there were only four units per building, Brian didn't feel moved to give an exact apartment number. Terry pulled into the first empty parking spot. It was the space located directly in front of Brian's apartment, his usual space. He couldn't help but wonder if it was a coincidence. Terry seemed to possess an uncanny ability to know everything about everyone.

"Thanks for the lift," Brian said, attempting to make his escape before the situation became any more awkward.

"Brian."

He froze with one foot on the pavement. The sound of his name falling from Terry's lips sent a shiver of longing down his spine. In an attempt to hide his reaction, Brian kept his movements slow as he turned his head, meeting Terry's gaze. With the interior light casting a glow across his features, Terry appeared twice as wicked.

He waited until Brian held his stare before saying anything else. A half-smile played across his lips and his eyes flashed with mischief as if he knew exactly the effect he had on Brian. "It was my pleasure." Damned if Brian could remember what they were talking about. Terry apparently understood and took mercy on him. "I'll see you at ten."

Rendered mute, Brian nodded before slipping from the truck. It wasn't until the door to his apartment closed behind him, sealing him inside the safety of his space and away from Terry's knowing gaze that Brian realized something important—he'd been played by a master. Terry had used every weapon in his arsenal to secure Brian's agreement and he'd allowed it to happen. Nothing good could come of this.

* * * * *

Against his better judgment, Brian presented himself at exactly ten a.m. at the address provided. One look at Terry's house reminded him of the many reasons why he wanted the title. It was huge and cool as hell. Even though he thought he didn't care about the money, he did. He didn't expect he'd ever be heavyweight-champion-rich but he couldn't deny it would be nice to be out from beneath his mother's crushing medical bills. The everyday struggle to survive sucked ass. He almost made it to the etched-glass front door before it swung wide and Terry stepped out. Since Brian had been expecting a training session, he'd worn workout pants, a t-shirt and a light jacket. He felt a bit underdressed in the face of Terry's dark jeans, sweater, and wool coat.

"Are you ready?"

Brian debated the merits of being a smartass before simply nodding. He was quickly learning it didn't matter what he said anyhow. Terry would do as he pleased.

Without bothering to ask where they were going, he fell into step behind Terry on his way down the driveway. He nodded toward Brian's car.

"I told you you'd have your car back."

"So you did." It was all Brian could think to say as he followed Terry. The pale exterior of Terry's home might have captured Brian's eye under different circumstances. He did catch a glimpse of glimmering pool water through the bushes surrounding the back yard. It also didn't escape his notice that Terry possessed not one, but three additional vehicles inside his garage. Two of them were classics worth more than Brian's entire life. All of those things would've held his attention any other time but it wasn't happening with Terry there. In comparison to the man leading him to the same truck he'd been in the night before, there was none.

"I have a few errands."

The remark effectively distracted him. "I thought we were training."

"I never said as much."

That brought Brian up short. Climbing into the passenger side, he went over the conversation they'd had the night before. Well shit. Terry hadn't specifically said they'd be working out. He'd alluded to it but nothing more. If Brian intended to survive this man, he would have to stay on his toes.

His confusion over Terry's intentions grew when their first stop turned out to be a florist. Since he didn't have a choice, Brian tagged along as Terry headed inside. An overenthusiastic saleswoman met them at the door. Her luminous smile spoke volumes about how happy she was to have Terry's business. Of course, Brian didn't miss the way she tugged subconsciously at her dark sweater before fluffing her brown hair. He half-expected her to adjust her cleavage at any moment.

"Terry!"

Brian cringed at the high-pitched squeal. Terry's face softened as if seeing an old friend. "Hey Betty. How's Anna doing this week?"

At Terry's question, the woman's features shifted and Brian caught a glimpse of a different side of her. He was suddenly reminded of his mother before her death. Betty had the same glint of exhaustion in her eyes.

She made a helpless gesture. "We're having an off week. They started her on a new medication and it's not working as well as they hoped. On the upside, we were approved for a new insurance plan. It won't help with the bills we already have but it should keep us from digging any deeper."

"That's awesome news about the insurance. I do hate that she's backsliding in her treatment. I know the doctors are always searching for better results but that doesn't make it any easier."

As the pair continued their discussion, Brian trailed away to inspect the tiny shop. Any time someone discussed health issues, he felt like an intruder on something personal. Not to mention, years of caring for a dying parent had left him drained. He did gather from their conversation that Anna was Betty's daughter and she had some form of cancer. The idea made him sad so he chose to concentrate on his surroundings instead. The scent of fresh-cut flowers hung heavily in the air. He didn't know much about such things, but several of the arrangements were nice to look at. He'd have to keep this place in mind.

"I'm sorry. I'm being rude. This is Brian," Terry said, pulling him out his musings. "Brian this is Betty Davenport." Brian dipped his chin in acknowledgment.

"It's nice to meet you," he responded automatically. She blushed, but didn't respond.

"Brian is McKenna's best friend," Terry added. The remark seemed to loosen her tongue.

"Oh, yay. I admit I'm running out of delivery ideas. Which flower do you think Terry should send McKenna this week?"

He shrugged as he nodded toward a nearby arrangement. "That one is nice." The pair stared at him as if he'd lost his mind.

"Hmm. Well. Let's get out my floral book and see what we can find," Betty suggested. They both dismissed him. After a few minutes of bending over the well-worn pages, Brian caught on. It seemed Terry had been sending McKenna different flowers for a long time. Sometimes he sent the same thing but included a different poem or comparison to her personality. It was a nice thing to do for his brother's widow. Of course, it wasn't lost on Brian how the orders also financially helped a woman with a chronically ill child. No doubt, Terry could afford simply to give the woman the funds needed for her daughter's care. Instead, he chose to spare her pride while giving her someone to talk to about her burden. Terry was wonderful.

*

With one errand down, Terry headed for his second home. Vegas Veteran's Rehabilitation Center could almost take first spot if he added up the number of hours he spent there each week. It wasn't as if he couldn't find anything better to do with his time, except there wasn't anything better anyone could be doing with their time. The men there were like his family. Of course, today he had an ulterior motive. The man silently riding shotgun didn't think he could come back from his injuries. Terry wanted to inspire him. More than that, he wanted Brian to know him. Not many people did. The fact that McKenna had seen something in the man told Terry a lot. Everyone loved McKenna but she didn't bother with people unless there was a good reason. Terry was intrigued.

Very few people in the world were innately good. From what Terry had witnessed so far, Brian was one of them. He deserved another shot at the top. Terry liked when nice guys finished first. It just so happened he was in the position to give him a leg up. Terry showed him around, pointing out a few of the latest designs in medical care for amputee patients. After a few introductions, Brian's natural ability to get along with others kicked in. Terry timed his attack perfectly, waiting until the entire tour was complete and Brian was happily chatting away with Terry's usual sparring partner, Cameron North. In spite of all adversity, Cameron had risen above the extensive injuries he'd received while on deployment. He was the perfect example of "if he can do it then you can too" that Terry wanted Brian to see.

The moment there was a break in the conversation, Terry cut in. "This is where you'll be training from now on." He wasn't disappointed. Brian's jaw clenched.

"I've already said thanks but no thanks."

"It wasn't a question."

He could see Cameron out of the corner of his eye shifting nervously. "I guess that's my cue. It was nice meeting you, Brian." Brian's gaze shifted to Cameron. After a quick handshake, he left them alone. When Brian focused on Terry once more, he didn't say a word, but there wasn't a need. His fury was evident in the muscle continuing to flex in his jaw. Terry wasn't backing down.

"As much as I like Rhys and all the guys at No Rival, they are your competition. If you hope to topple their reign, you can't keep expecting them to teach you how." He could see Brian searching for a response. He didn't want to hear it. Pride was the only thing holding the man back.

"Some of us have to work for a living."

"What does that have to do with anything?"

A look of confusion passed over Brian's face before he answered. "I can't ditch No Rival. They sign my paycheck." When Terry continued staring at him without speaking, Brian sighed. "I'm a fitness instructor," he added, obviously misunderstanding the reason for his silence.

"What does that have to do with

anything?" Terry repeated.

"I guess nothing." Brian couldn't have sounded more petulant if he tried.

A triumphant smile stretched Terry's lips. He couldn't hide his reaction, nor did he wish to do so. Cockiness was one trait he possessed in droves. It was best Brian accept it now. Otherwise, this would be a miserable experience for the man. "Good. Don't forget how we got here. You'll be seeing quite a bit of this place."

"So, they'll let me start training in a government-run facility with no questions? Seems logical."

He was a smartass. Terry liked it. "You'll come and go as you please. It's my money funding this place not the government. As for tomorrow—"

"Is there any charity you're not funding? Between you and Drew, there shouldn't be anyone left in need," Brian said, interrupting him.

"It's not charity. These men earned the right to be here and it's not as if I built the place. The government intended to shut this program down two years ago due to budget cuts and I stepped in. With the help of some awesome business professionals who run private charities for a living, we've managed to keep the doors open. Now, as for our next session, be at my house at seven p.m. Friday and we'll start lesson two."

"I don't remember having a lesson one."

Terry held his gaze, needing Brian to understand how serious he was. "Lesson one—I always get what I want."

Chapter Two

"I don't understand how this is supposed to help me in a sanctioned bout," Brian said as they pushed their way through the crowded entryway at Warehouse District. The place was famous for its weekend no-holds-barred underground MMA matches. Unlike World Divisional where a list of regulations kept fighters somewhat safe, these men entered the arena with only one rule—to the death. The bets were high and the money was phenomenal but you might not make it out once you entered the octagon.

"You have heart and I can make sure you have the skills needed to get the top, but these men," Terry said, indicating the two men currently pounding away at each other on the mat. "They have brute force. You need to learn to appreciate the fundamentals. If you take what you already know, mix it with what I can teach you, and learn to harness what these men have, you'll be unstoppable."

The two men inside the cage were friends. They were also equal in strength and ruthlessness. Brian would know. One of the men was Kurt Travis—the man who'd thrown a major wrench in his career by snapping his arm the only time they'd faced off on the mat. His opponent Knox Collier was a Warehouse District favorite. He was also the brother of the man who currently held the middleweight title.

Judging by the amount of sweat covering each man's body, they'd been at it awhile. Blood ran down one of Knox's cheeks but he didn't seem to notice. Brian couldn't believe either man was still standing since it was obvious they'd both taken a pounding.

"It won't be long now. Pick your winner."

Brian thought it over, measuring both men before making his decision. "Kurt. He's the stronger of the two."

Knox faked a kick and in a flash of movement, he pulled off the perfect superman punch. It was over. Terry leaned close to his ear. "Be thankful you didn't face him that night instead of Kurt." Brian saw his point but the outcome of the match still surprised him.

"I never saw that coming," Brian said.

Terry didn't respond. Brian glanced over. He was closer than he expected and completely unreadable. Brian did his best to stay on topic with Terry crowding his body and thoughts. "If this was a lesson in strength, I think your plans were ruined by the outcome." To his surprise, Terry chuckled.

"Lesson two—crazy trumps strength every damn time. Kurt has some dark places in his mind. They make him dangerous. Knox is broken. It makes him deadly. Never step in the cage with someone crazier than you are. That's where you went wrong the night you challenged Kurt. He's not better than you. He's unbalanced."

*

Terry had a great time with Brian. The man kept him on his toes. Every lesson he attempted to teach Brian, the man made him work for. He didn't take anything at face value without an explanation. It was refreshing and challenging. Brian stimulated him on every level. That was one of the biggest reasons Terry was now plying him with alcohol. If the man had one weakness, it was his complete

37

inability to hold his liquor. Terry wasn't sure any longer if this was lesson three or if he hoped Brian's effect on him would dim once he became inebriated. It wasn't happening. In fact, the more Brian relaxed in Terry's presence, the sexier he became. Perhaps it hadn't been the brightest move for Terry to choose to do this at his house, but he wanted this to be a controlled experiment.

He kept Brian's glass full. Anyone else might think this was a ridiculous bit of mentality training. Unfortunately, judging by the last time Brian had gotten drunk, he was a reckless drinker. Brian needed to either become accustomed to its effects or learn to say no. When he took to the road for competitions, the temptation to join every party would be massive. He couldn't do stupid shit...such as jumping a fence and slicing open his femoral artery the way he'd done with McKenna.

"I never drink and you plan to make me drink alone?"

A grin tugged at Terry's lips at Brian's sullen comment. "You need the fortification while I've had more than my fair share for one lifetime."

Brian's speech was already beginning to slow down. "It's not right to leave a man hanging."

"I have to drive you home and I don't drink and drive."

Brian slipped down an inch in his chair. Crossing his arms over his chest, he stared at Terry through his lashes. "I could stay here." Although Terry doubted Brian's proposition was intended the way he would've liked, it still caused his cock to lengthen. "It wouldn't be the first time I slept in a chair." That statement might have taken the bite out his arousal if

Brian's tone hadn't gone sultry. Not to mention, his eyes darkened. Terry shifted in his seat to hide his erection. The expression Brian wore was hot as hell.

"I wouldn't let you sleep in a chair." He hoped Brian was now wondering where he would allow him to sleep. Of course, the answer was nowhere. If Brian stayed, neither of them would get any rest.

Brian tossed back another shot before straightening in his seat. "If I'm not staying then I'd better go home. I'd hate to pass out on you and like I said, I don't drink often."

With a nod, Terry stood. Brian attempted to follow suit but swayed on his feet. Racing forward, Terry caught him before he could hit the ground. The motion left them chest to chest. A nervous sounding chuckle vibrated from Brian. Terry could feel it against his skin. Their gazes met. The sound died.

"You're very bossy," Brian said, surprising a chuckle from Terry. "You're very drunk," Terry countered.

Brian didn't move away. Neither did Terry. "I'll get over being drunk, you'll always be bossy."

"I have a feeling—if you remember any of this tomorrow—you'll be horrified."

Brian was staring at his mouth. He shook his head. "Nope. I haven't done anything to be embarrassed about...yet."

Terry marveled over the way Brian's eyes gave away his every emotion. They seemed to flash from light to dark brown and back again as he visibly struggled against his desire. Unable to keep from doing so, Terry gave him an extra shove. Using his voice against him, he allowed a hint of his growing lust to seep into his tone.

"Do you intend to?" With his gaze still locked on Terry's mouth, Brian nodded. "Do it," Terry taunted. The words barely passed his lips before Brian claimed his mouth. For Terry, it was like tossing gasoline on an already raging bonfire. It was everything he'd fantasized it would be with an extra helping of expertise tossed into the mix. The way Brian's tongue stroked the roof of his mouth before slipping away and reappearing again left Terry with no choice except to chase after it. The moment he thought he had him, Brian sank his teeth into Terry's bottom lip, tugging gently. Terry gasped. He couldn't remember a time he'd been this close to coming in his jeans, especially from nothing more than a kiss. At the sound, Brian turned his face away, resting his forehead on Terry's shoulder. His shoulders heaved as he visibly struggled to catch his breath.

"The room is spinning."

Terry clamped his back teeth together. His muscles seized tight as he attempted to control his lust. "That's because the world tilted," Terry said once he found his voice. An odd sense of chivalry overcame him. Brian was drunk. It was time for him to go home. Stepping out of his hold, Terry filled the shot glass to the brim before holding it out to Brian. "One more for the road. You know, to help steady the floor." Proving how inebriated he was, Brian seemed to find Terry's statement reasonable. He tossed it back. Terry sighed. "Come on. I'll take you home."

* * * * *

Brian had no idea what Terry had done to him the night before. Going by how his body felt, he suspected it involved several hours of licking envelopes while two sumo wrestlers sat on him. Even though he couldn't remember how he'd gotten home, flashes of Terry's hard chest against his as he ran his tongue along Brian's tongue kept invading his mind. Considering how badly he wanted him, Brian could only hope he'd kept those fantasies in his dreams and had not accosted the man. One thing he knew for sure was, he wouldn't have done such a thing sober since Terry didn't see him in that way. But the dream seemed so real. Even though he couldn't remember anything else about it other than the kiss, Brian was still so hard his dick was leaking onto his stomach. He could almost taste Terry, that's how realistic the picture was in his mind.

Settling back into his pillows, Brian focused on the opposite wall. The tiny yellow flowers and green sprigs covering his wallpaper stared back at him. He'd inherited a ton of debt when his mother passed away. Since he couldn't afford anything nicer than his current apartment, he was stuck with the outdated stuff for a while longer. No matter how hard he tried to concentrate on the mundane, his erection wouldn't subside. It didn't care that Terry didn't want him. Even half-dead from consuming way too much alcohol, he still craved Terry's touch.

Brian couldn't claim there was merely something about the man he couldn't resist. It was everything about him. Terry appealed to him on every level. If forced to narrow it down to one quality, he'd choose confidence. Terry possessed it in droves. The way he smirked each time he ordered Brian around, it was the one-two punch. Confidence paired with Alpha.

Goose bumps rose on his skin at the thought. The muscles in his stomach tightened. Fuck. He wanted him. There were people he could call. It wasn't as if he didn't have options, if he wanted to spend the day in bed. But no one else would do. His hand headed south. A picture of Terry's green eyes settled in his mind. His eyes fell closed. He slipped his hands past the waistband of his jeans. He and Terry were chest to chest inside Brian's mind.

Encircling his swollen member, he squeezed. Their lips collided. Brian leapt from the bed, headed for the dresser, stripping as he went. The moment he was nude, he dug around inside his sock drawer until he found what he needed. Returning to the bed, he slid between the sheets once more. Determined to have Terry—even if it was only in his imagination—Brian squeezed his eyes closed. The image of Terry reappeared as clear as if he was actually there. It was a testament to how closely Brian watched the man's every action. He could recreate Terry behind his closed lids without omitting a single detail.

Drawing his knees up, Brian allowed them to fall open. His fingers traced every vein in his cock while picturing Terry's tongue doing the same. Cupping his balls, he did his best to alleviate the heaviness growing there. The muscles in his shoulders tightened. He imagined it was Terry spreading his legs wider. Toying with the spot between his scrotum and asshole with one hand, he fisted his erection with the other. A drop of pre-cum escaped. Capturing it with the tip of his finger, Brian smeared it over his hole before reaching for the toy he'd fetched from his dresser.

The picture in his mind changed. Terry was holding his gaze as his dick slid inside Brian. He mimicked the fantasy with the anal plug. His body took over, drawing it inside. He tugged at his cock, almost desperate for it to be real. His ass pulled greedily at the plug. Brian struggled for air as his hips left the bed, moving against the pumping of his dick. Pressure built at the base of his cock. Terry increased the pace. As hot semen exploded across his abdomen, hitting him in the chest, Brian called Terry's name. Brian was almost sick in that moment. The idea of never having Terry was devastating in its power. His cell phone rang. Crumpling the sheet between his fingers, he dragged the material across his stomach and chest, attempting to wipe away the evidence. When he rolled to his side, the plug hit his prostate causing him to moan. He spotted Terry's name on the face of his phone and he quickly answered.

"Hey." Damn. He could hear the desire in his own voice. He bit back a groan. A moment of silence filled the air before Terry responded.

"Good to know you're still alive."

Brian pressed his free hand into his eye socket attempting to control his reaction to hearing the man's voice so close on the heels of his fantasy. He cleared his throat. "Was there a chance I wouldn't be?"

"I was worried I'd poisoned you. By the time we made it to your house you were pretty out of it."

Awesome. He always ended up looking like an ass. "Sorry about that—"

Terry cut him off. "Why? I'm the one who kept your glass filled."

He could hear the smile in his voice. Brian snuggled deeper into his pillows. "In that case, I'm not sorry." A low rumble of laughter teased his ear. Closing his eyes, Brian drew a slow breath in through his nose. He wanted to hear the sound again. "I'm such a lightweight when it comes to alcohol," he said to keep the conversation going.

"That's a good thing. It shows strength of character."

"Yeah. Well," Brian said noncommittally. "I hope I didn't make too big of an ass of myself." Another rumble of laughter caressed his eardrum.

"You did make me swear I wouldn't tell a soul you'd been a fat kid with braces."

Brian covered his eyes with his free hand while doing his best to keep the embarrassment from showing in his voice.

"Hey. That's top secret stuff. You could ruin me with information like that."

"Sweet. Blackmail-worthy goods. I have you right where I want you now. Well...not right where I want you." The statement hung between them for a moment. Brian held his breath. "I'll have that when you show up here Monday for your first real training session."

Even though Brian had known he'd been reading too much into Terry's statement, it seemed hope did indeed spring eternal. He was still hanging on the man's every word while fantasizing he'd meant to have him a different way.

"I'll be there with bells on."

Chapter Three

So, it began. There was no other way Brian could think to describe the torment named Terry. His life was completely intertwined with the sexy ex-champ. Friday nights were reserved for watching the fights. Saturday mornings they visited with Betty and ordered McKenna's flowers for the week. Mondays and Wednesdays they sparred with the veterans. Tuesdays and Thursdays were two of his biggest ordeals. Those were spent training—in private—at Terry's house. Brian left each session with every muscle in his body on fire, especially his cock. When it came to the actual training, there were times Brian almost felt as if he was cheating on his regular trainer, Rhys. No matter how hard he tried, he couldn't stay away from Terry. On the plus side, Brian also couldn't deny the strength in his arm was returning thanks to Terry. Unfortunately, Brian wasn't sure if it was due to their usual sparring sessions or being forced to jack off daily if he didn't want to go insane.

Today was one of the torturous days they spent alone in the man's home gym. It was really more of a basement with foam flooring and a few exercise machines. Terry had managed to dig up some extra padding for the center of the room to keep them from killing one another. The lack of audience always seemed to make Brian's lust ten times its usual potency. The epic burst of testosterone had him working twice as hard. Only after an inch of sweat covered Brian did Terry call for a break. Leaning against the wall, he accepted a cold bottle of water, grateful for the solid surface at this back keeping him upright.

"Why didn't you challenge Rhys?"

Brian asked as soon as he caught his breath. Turning up his water bottle, he gulped down half the contents before clarifying. "I mean a second time. You're awful young for retirement and from what I can tell from our sessions, you have a much better shot at taking the title back than I have at ever winning it."

"I want things."

Terry's vague answer didn't make any sense as far as Brian was concerned. He winked. "I'd really like a million dollars."

He snorted at Brian's remark. Puffing out his cheeks, Terry set his fists on his hips and slowly released his breath. "I needed to mourn my brother without a picture of it landing on the six o'clock news." He swiped his hand across his eyes as if the subject exhausted him. When he dropped it back to his side, Terry seemed even more somber than usual. "MMA isn't the same as any other sport. If you're not on top, then nobody gives a shit about you or knows your name. As much as I loved competing, I missed having a political opinion, bitching openly about my stance on gun laws," he paused, meeting Brian's gaze with a smirk. "I really yearned to fuck someone without it being a matter of public debate." He spread his arms wide. "I thought I wanted fame. Turns out, I don't. It doesn't mean shit. When the world lost Gray, it lost one of the greatest men ever born and no one knew his name. I want to be that person."

It made sense. Brian didn't necessarily care for the fame aspect either. For him, it was more of a personal journey. Sometimes people didn't know what they really needed until they had everything they thought they wanted. From what

Brian knew about Gray from McKenna, Terry did aspire to greatness. Since Gray had died right before Terry lost the title and decided to retire, it fit that he would be ready for some peace.

"Am I a part of your plan to achieve sainthood?" Brian wanted to bite off his tongue the moment the question left his lips and the same thought he always had while in Terry's presence ran across his mind once more. No good could come of this.

"I don't know about sainthood but you're definitely part of my plan." There was something in his tone. Brian wished he could force Terry to say more. Silence grew between them as Terry watched him from across the room. It was as if he expected Brian to say something profound. He'd gone completely still, making Brian wonder if he was holding his breath. It was odd. Brian craved even Terry's silence. It was ridiculous for anyone to long for anything as much as Brian did Terry. The man was unattainable. There had never been a single whisper of Terry being in a relationship with anyone. "Your head's not with me today," Terry said, finally seeming to accept Brian wouldn't speak up.

Pushing away from the wall, Brian tossed his water bottle in the trash. "My head is always with you," he said under his breath. Clearing his throat, he spoke a little louder. "Let's get back to work."

Shoving his mouthpiece in, they squared off. Terry's expression went blank, distracting Brian. Never one to miss taking advantage, Terry sprang forward, attempting a push kick. Brian blocked it at the last moment, sparing his ribs from the blow. With his mind back in the game, Brian used Terry's forward momentum against him. Snagging his upper body, he snaked his knee through Terry's legs, hooking his ankle, intent on taking him to the mat. Unfortunately, Terry was still one step ahead of him. Rocking back on his heels, Terry spun in Brian's arms, pressing his back against Brian's chest. Even though he should've seen the man's next move coming, Brian couldn't think past the sensation of Terry's ass grinding against his cock. It would be so easy to touch his lips to the side of Terry's neck or use a bodylock for takedown. The world tilted. The floor raced upward, smacking him between the shoulder blades. The air whooshed from his lungs. Brian blinked at the ceiling in confusion for a moment before Terry's face blocked out the sight. He wasn't even short of breath as he hovered over him.

There wasn't a hint of triumph or disappointment in his expression. He was unreadable as he eyed Brian.

"Don't let me undermine you, because I will."

For some reason Brian couldn't explain, it seemed to him Terry wasn't talking about their match. Spitting out his mouth guard, Brian chuckled. "I'm waiting until you're overly confident."

A low rumble sounded from deep inside Terry's chest as he pulled Brian to his feet. "I'm always overconfident."

Brian clung to Terry's hand long after he should've released him. He held his stare. "One day soon, you won't know what hit you."

Terry smirked but he didn't let go or look away. "That's also already true."

Brian moved an inch closer. "Just so you know, even though I wasn't really joking about the million dollars, there's things I want too."

Terry's cock was screaming for attention. The expression Brian wore was devastating to Terry's heart. He didn't think the man was truly aware of how he was looking at him, but damn. His half-lidded eyes and tiny knowing grin called to Terry. To keep from doing something he couldn't take back, he hooked Brian's ankle with his foot and took the man down. He made sure to keep his strength in check. Following him to the floor, he pinned him to the mat. If it had been a real match, it would've counted as a win. He carefully kept his arousal hidden. Brian didn't appear surprised in the least to find himself flat on his back. He held Terry's gaze steadily as if awaiting his next move.

"We all have certain objects we wish

to possess," Terry said, lowering his lids. He glanced at Brian's mouth, wishing he could taste him, if only one more time. "Things we can't have," he added. Pressing his palms flat against the floor on either side of Brian's head, he leaned an inch closer. Breathing in the man's scent, he finally pushed away from him, coming to his feet. All Brian needed to do was drop his gaze and he'd be staring at the line of Terry's erection. It wasn't as if he could hide his reaction to the man. He didn't look.

The moment Terry closed the door behind Brian, he headed for his bedroom and fell across his bed. He didn't kid himself. If he didn't find relief, he'd go insane. Tugging at the drawstring on his shorts, Terry set his erection free. It wouldn't take long. Brian had kept him poised on the edge of madness for too long.

He palmed his cock and his hips left the mattress to meet his stroke. His fist pumped in quick, precise movements, moving toward a fast release. An image of Brian filled his mind. The motion slowed. When it came to him, Terry didn't want to rush. The way Brian watched him from beneath his lashes, hunger etched in his every feature. That was the picture Terry held onto as he stroked his shaft. Tiny bursts of electricity tingled across his skin as the pleasure began at his toes, working its way higher. Pressure built along with the phantom sensation of Brian pressed against him. His speed increased once more as his skin tightened. As a hot streak of semen hit him in the chest, Brian's name left his lips.

* * * * *

"No practice today."

Something about the short text

nagged at the back of Brian's mind for the two hours he had left before his shift at No Rival ended. It wasn't until he found himself driving in the opposite direction of his apartment that he decided he had to seek Terry out. Terry was always demanding, expecting to get his way. This was different. Something was wrong. Brian didn't know how he knew. He didn't have any solid evidence to base his feelings on, but he had to check. The closer he got to Terry's house, the worse his sense of foreboding became.

He could hear music blaring inside the house from the driveway. Thankfully, he found the back door unlocked since there wasn't a chance in hell anyone would be able to hear him knocking over the sound. By the time he made his way down the stairs into the gym, Brian was cringing against the assault on his senses.

It was lucky Terry had owned one of the rare houses with a basement in Vegas. When he spotted Terry, his sense of dread became a full-blown panic. If the man noticed his presence, he didn't acknowledge it. Sweat poured down his bare back, adding to his already soaking-wet workout shorts. Bouncing on his toes, he landed blows to the punching bag with enough force Brian could hear Terry's fist connecting with the leather over the deafening music.

He'd been at it awhile. There was no way his shorts had become melded to his skin with sweat unless he'd been nonstop for a long time. Terry paused long enough to lift a bottle of Jack to his lips. There were only a couple inches of the amber liquid left. He would kill himself hydrating in such a way. Choosing a spot near the stairs, Brian sat on the floor with his back against the wall.

Rage hung in the air. Brian half expected a black cloud of smoke to roll off Terry's skin at any moment and choke them both. Instead, he continued his relentless attack on the defenseless bag. In an attempt to stay calm, Brian tried to calculate the exact force of Terry's kicks and punches. He should have one of those sensors installed. It would be interesting to see the readings. For instance, Brian would love to know how they compared to the blow of a sledgehammer.

His musings managed to keep him distracted until Terry finished off the last of his whiskey. He stared at the bottle in his hand as if wondering where its contents had gone before hurling it against the wall with enough force that it shattered. Brian was a bit impressed. It was damn hard to smash a liquor bottle.

They were built to withstand drunkards. Thankfully, the concrete walls of the basement were too.

Chest heaving, Terry turned. Their gazes collided. Brian held his breath. The look in Terry's eyes scared the hell out of Brian. Terry was half-crazed.

"What the fuck are you doing here?" Terry barked, as he stormed across the room to tower over Brian. Considering his mood, Brian let him keep his height advantage.

"I was worried about you." He was forced to yell over the music to be heard. Terry narrowed his eyes before turning away long enough to slam his hand down on the sound system's power button. In a matter of seconds he was back to focusing his fury on Brian. In the wake of the sudden silence, Brian's ears rang as if he'd just left a concert.

"I told you not to come here."

Brian tried to keep his voice as calm as possible. "Technically, you didn't. You only said no practice."

Terry snapped. His fist struck the wall above Brian's head. "Don't give me that shit!"

Brian came to his feet. Somehow, he managed to hang onto his temper, but it was a near thing. Damn. Even wearing grappling gloves, Brian knew that shit had to have torn his knuckles to hell, but Terry didn't flinch. There was something else in his expression. The man was hurting. Brian hated it. "You can talk to me." Hearing the desperation in his voice, Brian paused reeling it back in before saying anything more. "Whatever it is, Terry. I'm here for you."

Closing his eyes, Terry tilted his head back. Regret etched his every line.

When he met Brian's gaze again, his eyes were almost pleading. "I can't." He shook his head. "I just can't."

It hurt. Brian couldn't lie. He would've preferred Terry hit him than hide things from him. The man didn't trust him. He couldn't fix that shit. "I see." There was no way anyone could've been more surprised by how steady he sounded than Brian. Inside, he was seething, but somewhere between his brain and tongue, it disconnected. "I guess there's nothing here for me then."

He moved to leave, determined to keep his shit together. He didn't make it two steps. Showing amazing reflexes for a man who'd consumed an entire bottle of whiskey, Terry snagged hold of Brian and he found his back against the wall before he realized he was no longer moving in the opposite direction. With his palm braced against the wall next to Brian, Terry kept his other hand flattened against the center of Brian's chest, holding him in place.

"So, what? You're just going to leave me?" Terry snarled. Brian didn't say a word, but a ridiculous burst of relief settled over him. Bowing his head, Terry stared at the floor. "Life is so goddamn unfair."

To Brian, it seemed Terry's words were meant more for himself. He dropped his hands and took a step back. Brian's heart fell. His chin lifted and Brian realized his eyes were swimming with unshed tears. Terry visibly swallowed. Brian couldn't fucking breathe. Terry was hurting and there was nothing he could do. Blinking rapidly, Terry finally focused on a spot over Brian's shoulder. He cleared his throat. His hands lifted, palms up, before falling back to his sides as if to say he had nothing. When he finally spoke, his voice came out sounding hoarse.

"Anna."

He stopped, obviously incapable of finishing. Brian was immediately grateful for the wall supporting him. It was no wonder Terry was such a mess. He wanted to help in any way he could.

"What can we do for Betty?"

At his question, Terry seemed to deflate. He pressed the heels of his hands against his eyes, swaying on his feet. Brian rushed forward, but Terry waved him away and stumbled up the stairs. Staying close on his heels, Brian did his best to ensure Terry didn't break his neck on the way up. As they passed through the kitchen, Brian caught a scent of lemons and disinfectant as if someone had recently cleaned. All the stainless steel appliances gleamed in the brightly lit room. The only thing marring the otherwise spotless room was the empty fifth of Crown sitting in the center of the island. Brian hadn't noticed it on his way in, which wasn't surprising since he was intent on finding Terry. Now, he wondered why Terry wasn't dead after consuming so much alcohol.

Terry didn't protest as Brian followed him down the hall and into his bedroom. A large flat-screen TV covered the wall beside the bathroom. Terry switched it on, flipping through the channels until he found a hockey game. It was a rerun but Brian didn't think Terry was truly aware of anything he was doing at this point. He was going through the motions. That was it. When he spoke, it surprised Brian how dead his voice had become.

"I need a shower." He passed Brian

the remote. "Don't go away, okay?"

At Brian's nod, Terry headed inside the bathroom, leaving the door slightly cracked behind him. Brian released a sigh of relief. If Terry crashed in the shower, he really didn't want to have to kick the door in. He glanced around the room trying to decide what to do. None of the furniture in Terry's bedroom appeared designed to be used for its intended purpose. It was all too nice. The dresser, chest of drawers, bureau and a bench at the foot of the bed were all oak, but the tops looked to be made out of marble. It sort of threw him. Even though he was somewhat certain the bench was meant to be used as such, he didn't want to break anything. Giving up, he sat on the bed. His ass sank into the mattress.

"What the hell?"

He poked it. The indention slowly

dissipated. Okay. That was cool. He did it again. This time, he realized it was also unnaturally cool to the touch. Before he could change his mind, Brian toed off his shoes and settled in. It was awesome. Turning on his side, he pillowed his head with his hands and stared at the TV. His chest hurt. Terry had been helping Betty for so long. It must seem as if he'd lost a member of the family or worse, as if he'd failed her in some way. Grief was funny like that. It didn't care about the truth. Brian understood more than most. Life was nothing more than long spells of dealing with death and bullshit occasionally interrupted by short bursts of happiness. For someone such as Terry, someone genuinely good, it would be even worse. Empathy was a motherfucker. The heartless had it easy.

Even though Brian kept his gaze

locked on the men skating across the ice, he was completely focused on every sound coming from inside the bathroom. When the door finally swung wide and Terry reappeared, Brian's shoulders relaxed. He hadn't realized how tense he'd become until that moment.

A dark blue towel hung low on Terry's hips. His wet hair was slicked back, away from his face, leaving every chiseled line visible. As Brian looked on, a drop of water slid down Terry's bare chest. Brian tore his gaze away. Terry was every bit as covered as he'd been before his shower. If Brian was being honest with himself, the towel probably hung even lower than his shorts had. That detail didn't matter in the least. There was something about knowing one tiny tug would be all it would take to have Terry right where he wanted him. Was it a bad time? Hell yeah, but his heart didn't care.

If Terry was the least bit concerned over Brian being in his bed, he didn't show it. As he stumbled toward the edge, Brian realized he obviously didn't intend to put any fucking clothes on. Terry set one knee on the mattress next to him. Brian's thoughts scattered in every direction. He scrambled to decide what he was supposed to do. Should he scoot over? Sit up? Run for his life? The final one seemed a solid plan. In the end, he did none of those things. Showing an impressive amount of skill for a drunk man, Terry began climbing over Brian while still managing to hold onto his towel. Brian rolled with him. He was completely helpless to stop it as Terry used Brian's chest to steady himself. He hovered above him for a second. Their gaze met. Terry's was hooded. Brian's mind ceased working.

"Don't move."

Brian held still at the order, not even daring to breathe. "I am."

Terry dove-fell face first into the spot next to him on the bed. "Could've fooled me," he grumbled into the mattress. "Whole goddamn room is spinning." Brian stared hard at the ceiling unable to as much as look at the man beside him. "You won't go away, will you?"

"I won't go away," Brian promised.

"Funeral's tomorrow."

"You won't be alone," Brian assured him.

"Thank you for showing up."

Brian finally turned his head, bringing Terry into focus. His eyes were closed and his breathing was steady. "There's nowhere I'd rather be." Brian had never meant anything more in his life.

* * * * *

Anna's funeral was every bit as hard as Terry feared. Betty held up well, but he wasn't fooled. She would have a rough road ahead of her. The loss of his brother still sneaked up on him, punching him in the throat at times he least expected. The all too familiar feeling of helplessness overwhelmed him. He would've never survived the day without Brian at his side. The man was something special, no doubt about it.

When the time came for the first handful of dirt to be tossed onto the casket, Terry walked away. It was the one thing he couldn't do. Even though he moved in the opposite direction of the truck, Brian followed without question. With no real plan to do so, he ended up sitting on the stone bench at the foot of Gray's grave. He made sure to leave enough room for Brian. Taking the hint,

Brian sat at his side. Terry stared at his brother's name etched in stone.

"Who takes care of you?" Terry wasn't sure where the question had come from, but suddenly he realized he really wanted to hear Brian's answer.

"What do you mean?"

Terry shrugged. "McKenna says you took care of her after the whole Kurt debacle. Now, you're here with me. Who does this for you?"

Brian stared off in the distance. He seemed to take the question seriously, giving it careful thought before answering. "If you'd asked me that a few months ago, I would've said I take care of me."

"What happened a few months ago?"

"I met you."

Terry stared at Brian's profile willing him to meet his gaze. He needed to see his eyes. Brian didn't look. Instead, he nodded toward Gray's grave.

"What was he like? I mean, I've heard McKenna's version of him but what's yours?"

It was for the best. Hurting Brian wasn't something he ever wanted to do. Openly loving him could only destroy him. Terry allowed the change in topic to stand.

"He was wicked, in intelligence and sense of humor. There wasn't a single topic he didn't know at least a little something about. If he couldn't charm someone with his genius, he'd have them rolling with laughter at his bawdy sense of humor." An image of Gray came to life in Terry's mind and he smiled in spite of himself. "It only took one look at him to see his mind was always on the move, calculating every situation." Terry snorted. "The funny thing is, for the most part I'm not surprised he was too much for this world. McKenna is the only exception to that statement. When it came to her, he was completely human. She reduced him to the basest of males and it was a beautiful thing. It was also hilarious to watch." Terry chuckled at the memory. "I'd never seen him blush or stutter before her. After her, he was a complete mess." Terry's smile fell. No one ever asked him about Gray. He hadn't realized how much he felt robbed for it. Brian gave him the chance to share him, keeping his memories alive. "Thank you."

Brian glanced over. A flash of surprise crossing over his features. "For what?"

"Putting up with me," Terry answered without hesitation.

With a snort, Brian looked away. "Yeah, well, I'm pretty sure I gave you my social security number before confessing I'd been a fat kid with braces that night you got me drunk, so you know"—he shrugged—"you could steal my identity or some shit."

Terry's breath caught in his throat. He eyed Brian's profile, searching for any sign he remembered more about that night than he'd let on. When he didn't respond, Brian turned his head again, meeting his gaze. His expression was clear of any hint of emotion, and Terry released his pent-up breath.

"I have had my eye on a Neiman Marcus gold card." When Brian smiled, the heavy weight that had been sitting on Terry's chest since learning of Anna's death, lifted a bit. If they were never more than they were right now, he would still be a better man for having met Brian.

* * * * *

Although it was Wednesday and they were spending the day sparring with the vets, Brian couldn't take another minute of temptation. Since the night he'd spent sleeping at Terry's side a week ago, he'd been unable to think about anything else. It had bordered on torture. When he'd slipped out of the bed for a trip to the bathroom the next morning, Terry had still been sleeping soundly but when he'd returned Terry had been gone. After a short search, he'd found him with his head stuck in the freezer, searching for something to fix them for breakfast. He'd never said a word about that night and Brian didn't either. But it was there, sitting in between them.

Thankfully, Brian's first match was in two days. He wouldn't be forced to endure another day alone with Terry due to pre-bout weigh-ins. In an act of pure desperation, Brian invited McKenna to join them for their usual morning routine with the promise of buying her lunch afterward. He hoped her presence would blunt the impact of Terry. It didn't work.

"Again!" Terry yelled, tugging Brian to his feet. Circling him on the mat, all of Brian's building frustration rushed to the surface, hitting its breaking point. Without any real intent in doing so, he shot forward, kicking out. He swept Terry's feet out from beneath him. Without waiting for him to recover, Brian followed him down. Terry scrambled to avoid him but wasn't quick enough. In his attempt to get away, Terry ended up flat on his stomach when Brian pinned him to the mat. In spite of his inability to break Brian's hold, he laughed. Triumph heavily laced the sound. Even though they were practicing, Terry still observed the rules, tapping out. The moment Brian's hold slackened, Terry rolled over onto his back. A luminous smile pulled at his lips. With his chest heaving from his attempt to catch his breath, Terry's eyes shone in his happiness. Brian couldn't look away.

"If I still held the title—that would've been your moment. Can you imagine? You'd be holding the world right now."

He already was.

"Until Friday night," Terry said, pushing himself from the floor. Brian's gaze followed him all the way to the locker room until he disappeared inside.

"He wants to fuck you."

Still half-upright from his attempt to stand, Brian whipped around at McKenna's statement. The motion left him off balance. Lights popped behind his eyes. "What?" There was a moment, even as he watched her wave away his question, where he wondered if it had been him asking the question. The growl seemed over-the-top even to his ears.

"The last I checked we still spoke the same language. Terry desires you in a sexual way," McKenna clarified as if he didn't understand the word "fuck".

"That's ridiculous."

Ever the intellect, McKenna tilted her head to one side, studying him. "Why? You're attractive. That mocha skin tone coupled with your gorgeous eyes is a hell of a combination. Not to mention, you're also the nicest person I've ever met. It makes sense he'd be drawn to you. The need to possess someone equal in strength is fairly common."

Brian shook his head. "In what world does that make sense? I don't know the percentages or anything, but it's not typical for a man to want another man sexually."

She blinked owlishly as if he was the one speaking a foreign language. "Now who's being ridiculous?"

He opened his mouth to respond. Nothing came out. Snapping his teeth together, he considered her words. Was he being blind? No. He didn't believe so. "I stand by my statement. It's not typical."

McKenna seemed to consider his words again before responding. "Well. I'm not sure what the actual numbers are, but in this case, Terry is gay. Therefore, I imagine the odds swing in your favor."

Once again, the world seemed to tilt on its axis. "What?"

McKenna nodded as if it had been a yes or no question. "I assumed you knew as much since you've been eating him alive with your eyes."

"What?" He repeated, for lack of

anything more intelligent to say. Surely, he would've heard something before now. People in Terry's position couldn't avoid gossip. Even if such a thing wasn't substantiated, there would've been rumors, whisperings.

"Please tell me you don't need me to explain the mechanics?" McKenna's dryly spoken question pulled him from his thoughts.

"Of course not."

"Then I don't understand your problem." She lifted one shoulder. "He wants you. You obviously want him too." She shrugged again. "Oh look, there's Cameron. I'll go say hi while you change."

She trailed away leaving him alone with his thoughts. As Terry's sister-in-law, McKenna would know more about the man's personal life than anyone would. It wasn't as if he could call her a liar.

Inside the locker room, Brian sat down on the bench, staring at his bag. He peeled his sweat-soaked shirt over his head and wiped his face with it. With his mind on other things, it took a minute for the sound of sloshing water to penetrate his brain. Shifting positions, he peeked around the edge of the cabinets. The showers came into his line of sight. He regretted it immediately. With a large gap between the wall and curtain, he had a clear view of Terry. With his head tilted back, rinsing the shampoo from his hair, his entire body was bared to Brian's gaze. He turned away immediately, not wanting to get busted ogling the guy, but damn. The image was now burned into his mind. It was every bit as delicious as he'd suspected. He couldn't move. His dick was too hard. It paralyzed him. Never had he wanted anyone the way he did Terry. The knowledge solidified a decision for him. It had been growing for a while now. After his first fight, he wouldn't train with Terry any longer.

In spite of what McKenna had said, Terry hadn't given him any real reason to hope the desire was mutual. He'd been nothing but good to Brian. There had been times when he thought he'd seen something in the man's eyes. Most likely, it was wishful thinking on his part. This couldn't continue. He'd experienced too many setbacks and losses already. Ruining his friendship with Terry and McKenna wasn't an option.

"You look lost."

The sound of Terry's voice broke through Brian's thoughts. With a white towel wrapped around his hips, Terry loomed over him. His upper body glistened with beads of water. Brian glanced away, fearing the hunger was written in every line on his face.

"Just worrying about this weekend," he lied. He was a tiny bit concerned, but it was more he didn't want to fail Terry than he cared about losing the match.

"Don't. I'll be at your side the entire time and I'm good luck."

Brian smiled in spite of himself. Before he could stop it from happening, he massaged the aching spot in the center of his chest.

"I guess I'd better let you get a shower. McKenna's probably starving and you know she's likely to forget to eat if someone doesn't make her," Terry said.

"Yeah," Brian absently agreed. "I'd hate for Kurt to kill me for letting her wither away."

"He's not allowed to touch you." The fierce edge to Terry's tone caused Brian's head to snap around in his direction. The expression the man wore wiped Brian's mind blank. "Never again. Do you understand?" He really didn't, but he still nodded. "Good. I'll see you Friday night."

As Terry walked away, Brian realized something important. He was truly, totally and royally fucked. No one else would do because somewhere along the way, he'd lost his heart.

Chapter Four

Terry could tell Brian was pumped. It was written in every move he made. The past three months of hard training was showing itself now that his moment was finally here. He was staring down his opponent, obviously doing his best to psych out the other man as the outside referee did his final equipment check. Passing inspection, Brian made his way inside the octagon while holding his adversary's stare. The excitement of the crowd was almost tangible, their roar deafening. Between their raised voices, the commentators and the inside ref reading the rules, Terry could barely hear his own thoughts. He didn't dare look away from Brian. In some small way, he hoped it lent him strength. If nothing else, Terry needed him to know he was right there with him all the way.

He could've gone in as Brian's cornerman, but he worried he'd be more of a distraction than encouragement. The position was too important. Instead, Terry enlisted Cameron's help. Brian landed the blue corner since he was the less experienced of the two fighters and wasn't favored to win. It was Brian's first match since his injury. For that reason it seemed as if every one of his friends had turned up to show their support.

With the exception of McKenna, Terry ignored them all. Occasionally, he would wrap his arm around her waist to keep her from getting jostled by the crowd. Otherwise, he remained focused on Brian. He didn't imagine any of the No Rival gang was surprised by his neglect of them. Since his retirement, he'd withdrawn from everyone. Only McKenna and—he assumed—her husband Kurt knew the real reason why.

"This shit has too many rules," Kurt growled breaking into his thoughts. Even though it did seem to Terry as if it was taking an inordinate amount of time to get through them tonight, he felt the need to point out the obvious.

"Yeah. Well. You remember what happened the last time Brian fought without them." Kurt winced and Terry immediately regretted the words. During an underground and unsanctioned match, Kurt had been the one who'd broken Brian's arm, knocking him out of contention for the title on the legal circuit. Terry knew Kurt carried enough guilt without him adding to it. Before he could apologize, Knox appeared at Kurt's other side.

"Goddamn. Are they still reading the

fucking rules?"

Some of the tension left his shoulders. A chuckle slipped past his lips. It seemed he wasn't the only one on edge. Everyone understood how much was riding on this bout. Brian could recover from the loss, but for pride's sake, he needed to win.

McKenna snagged his attention. "Who is that guy prowling around the outside of the cage?" Following her line of sight, he spotted a man in his late forties wearing an expensive business suit. He paced the edge of the octagon, staring intently at everything happening on the mat.

"He's a World Divisional Exec," Terry explained. "They're at every match. At the end of the night, he'll determine how bonuses for such things as best submission of the night will be awarded."

The bell rang, and—thankfully—Rhys picked up the explanation. When McKenna's curiosity piqued she was full of endless questions. He couldn't concentrate.

Brian's challenger had a longer reach and more experience. There was no way he wanted it as badly as Brian did. Not to mention, he hadn't had Terry training him. A smirk touched Terry's lips. No. He wouldn't beat Brian. Biting back a laugh, he watched as the tattoo-covered man bounced around, attempting to draw Brian in. Other than the subtle shift of weight as Brian moved to the balls of his feet, he didn't react. Light glimmered off his freshly shaved head and the Vaseline on his cheeks. Even from this distance, Terry could see the way his eyes followed the man's motions, checking for weaknesses. Only because Terry had been sparring with Brian for weeks now did he see the strike coming. With panther-like grace, Brian leaped, striking the man in the side of the head. So, it began.

The match was set for five rounds at five minutes each and it went four. Terry thought he'd die of heart failure before Brian managed to snag hold of his rival's legs and take him to the mat for submission. Not until they announced Brian's name as the winner did Terry draw an easy breath. Unfortunately, the moment they did, a realization hit. Brian didn't need him any longer. Glancing around, he recognized his time was over. While everyone else rushed forward, hoping to congratulate Brian, Terry stole his chance and slipped away.

*

The faces of all the people he'd known since starting down this path, blurred before Brian's eyes. He knew it was the adrenaline pumping through his veins causing his inability to focus on any of them. With the exception of one glaring detail—Terry wasn't among them. His smile didn't dissipate. If there was one person in the world Brian could count on, it was Terry. Brian knew it in his gut. Wherever Terry had run off to, he'd find him. He hurried through the handshakes and congratulations in his rush to start his search. McKenna caught his eye and a silent message passed between them. In a dramatic move worthy of an Oscar, she slapped her hand to her forehead and swayed slightly, drawing everyone's attention her way.

"Whoa. I think I've had a bit too much excitement."

Brian could tell by the way Kurt's eyes flashed with humor that he saw right through McKenna's performance. Luckily, he didn't give her away and he seemed to be the only one. Not that Brian intended to give any of them time to think about it for long.

"You all should go. I still have a ton of shit to do before I can leave here."

Turning his face away from the others, Kurt visibly bit back a smile before he spoke. "We hate running out on you, but McKenna has been on her feet quite a bit today." At her husband's words, McKenna stroked his forearm as if silently praising him for standing by her story.

"Think nothing of it," Brian reassured him with a grateful smile. After a quick round of goodbyes, Brian rushed for the back of the building. The cool air of the dressing room hit his skin. He barely registered the drop in temperature with the adrenaline pouring through his veins.

Tilting his chin, Brian glanced around the room with new eyes, dragging a deep breath into his lungs. He was a winner again. A movement out of the corner of his eye caught his attention. He wasn't surprised to see Terry leaning against the counter beside the sink with one ankle crossed over the other and his arms overlapping his chest. Brian did his best not to draw notice to his actions as he snapped the lock in place behind his back. With that detail out of the way, he crossed the room. Terry didn't straighten from his relaxed pose until Brian was standing a foot away.

"I wondered where you'd disappeared to."

One corner of Terry's mouth turned upward. Brian focused on it. He always found the man's tiny smirk more desirable than the brightest of smiles from anyone else. "You didn't need me out there."

At the bullshit statement, Brian's gaze shifted. He held Terry's stare, hoping he would see the honesty behind his words. "I always need you."

"Nah. You had this in you all along. You would've eventually found it with or without me."

Brian shook his head. "That right there proves you're not really hearing me. You are necessary to me." Terry's lips parted in surprise but he didn't respond. Brian wasn't sure why he was determined to push things. Perhaps he was merely riding the high of his win. The only thing he knew for sure was he couldn't let Terry walk away from him tonight. Terry's usual mocking smile fell back into place.

"You're probably ready to get out of here and celebrate. I wanted to offer my congratulations before you disappeared."

With his compliments out of the way, Terry started past Brian, making for the door. Brian had an epiphany. All the things he'd feared, Terry had the same concerns. He didn't think Brian was truly interested in him. What an idiot.

He stepped into Terry's path, blocking him from leaving. One of Terry's eyebrows lifted in question. Brian was through talking, finished playing. Snagging Terry by the back of his neck, Brian hauled him forward. A small part of him still expected rejection. It didn't happen. He'd also considered the possibility he might fall on Terry like a starving dog by the time he finally got the chance to taste him. Instead, a sense of peace settled over him the second their lips met. Emotion bloomed from the center of his chest, stealing his breath as Terry's tongue touched his. The moment it did, a second wave of knowledge overcame Brian. They'd been here before. The erotic dream that had been haunting him since the night he'd passed out from drinking too much at Terry's house wasn't a dream at all.

Taking a step forward, he backed Terry against the counter's edge, trapping him. He'd escaped him once. Tonight, Brian was stone-cold sober. It wouldn't happen twice. Brian poured every ounce of skill he possessed into the kiss. When Terry moved to pull away, Brian followed, holding Terry's bottom lip between his for a moment longer before allowing Terry a bit of space. Terry held tight to Brian's waist as if incapable of completely letting the moment go. With his eyes closed and lips slightly parted, he visibly struggled for air. His flushed face and kiss-swollen mouth created the sexiest image Brian had ever seen. It did something to his stomach. His lids lifted. Brian's groin tightened. Lust mixed with something more shined out at him from Terry's gaze.

"I don't care to be just another part of your adrenaline rush."

"I don't want anyone else to be," Brian admitted. "There hasn't been anyone else since I set eyes on you in that hospital room. That's the biggest reason I didn't aspire to be your side project, a fixer-upper. I need you to see something more when you look at me."

Terry's eyes fell closed again for a moment before reopening. "I can't lie. Part of it was about fixing you."

His admission hurt more than Brian would've expected, but it didn't matter. It wasn't enough to make him back down. He'd wanted Terry for too long.

"Don't look at me like that," Terry

added, sounding desperate. "My goal was to help you regain your dream. It wasn't because you're some sad case who needs me. I needed you." His grip tightened at Brian's waist. "From the instant we met, you've been in my head." A smirk twisted his lips as he added, "Writhing and moaning beneath me."

Brian's cock lengthened, aching with need.

Terry's gaze dropped to Brian's mouth. "I've done things to you in my mind..." He paused, leaving Brian to guess what those things were. He had some ideas. He wanted to do them now. Then Terry's lids lifted and light-green eyes shining brighter than before stared at him with an intensity he'd never experienced. Every thought left his head with one look from Terry. "The thing is," Terry continued, his voice dropping to almost a whisper. "I've done things to you with my heart I didn't expect."

Brian held his breath, praying Terry wouldn't stop. Terry seemed to have the same reaction. He'd gone completely still in Brian's arms as if he feared his rejection. Recognizing the man expected him to make the next move, Brian cupped Terry's face between his hands, forcing Terry to hold his gaze. He slowly lowered his head, drawing out the moment. Pausing an inch from Terry's lips, Brian gave him the power to destroy him. "I love you." Terry closed the distance between them.

Wasting no time, Brian went straight for the button of Terry's jeans, freeing his erection. Tearing his mouth away, he sucked a deep breath in through his nose. As the silky skin brushed along his palm, he could almost feel Terry's gratification. He'd been waiting for so long to have him it was almost as if the pleasure was his. Without bothering to push his jeans past his hips, Brian went down on his knees. Skipping all niceties, he wrapped his lips around Terry's dick, growling as the man's flavor coated his tongue. Terry's knuckles whitened as he gripped the edge of the counter behind him, as if his knees would no longer fully support him. Closing his eyes against the sight, Brian opened his jaw wide, taking Terry to the back of his throat.

"Holy. Jesus. Fuck." Terry seemed to scramble for words as Brian hollowed out his cheeks. He was still too coherent as far as Brian was concerned. He wanted him incapable of speech. The thrumming of his own cock pushed against the waistband of his shorts, attempting escape. He ignored it. Right now, all Brian needed was everything Terry had to give. His pulse beat inside his ears from the force of the excitement racing through his veins. Male salt danced on his taste buds. His throat burned from the pounding of Terry's dick.

Even as Terry's ragged breathing filled the air, he snagged Brian beneath the arms, hauling him to his feet before he could finish the job. The man's tongue filled his mouth. He was everywhere. Brian's shorts loosened beneath Terry's touch. His cock cheered at the freedom. When Terry's hand closed around his erection, Brian swore stars exploded behind his closed lids. Terry's mouth moved to his jawline. He spoke against Brian's skin as he palmed him.

"There's a condom in my wallet. Get it." Brian fumbled to do as he bade. When he had it, Terry squeezed his cock, almost causing him to orgasm right then. "Put it on," Terry ordered, pushing his jeans down his hips as Brian moved to do as told. Terry's eyes seemed to flash even brighter than usual as he watched Brian with hooded lids. "I've been fantasizing about you fucking me for months now." The confession caused Brian's hands to tremble as he suited up. "Do it now."

At Terry's command, everything seemed to slow. Brian's breathing steadied. Being with Terry was right. The rushing panic to have him quickly, before the chance slipped him by, fell away. The world steadied. This man desired him every bit as badly as Brian wanted him. The knowledge was freeing. It allowed him to plan his next move methodically. The moment Terry kicked free of his clothing, Brian struck. Snagging the man's hips, he urged him higher. Holding one of Terry's legs to his side, he probed the entrance of Terry's ass. With nothing except a condom at his disposal, there was no way to make things easier. He tried going slow. The dazed expression Terry wore made it impossible. Easing inside an inch, Brian immediately retreated before returning. This time he went an inch deeper. Terry fisted his own cock and Brian dropped his chin to watch. The sight was so erotic, he couldn't hold back any longer. Without warning, he surged upward, impaling Terry. A moan came from deep within the man's chest. The sound caused Brian's balls to draw up tight. Long weeks of unfulfilled desire rose to the forefront, punching Brian in the gut. A combination of the vision of his cock pumping inside Terry and the sounds of his sighs had an orgasm rising to the tip of his dick.

A cry ripped from Terry's throat as a

jet of semen landed across his abs. It was too much for Brian. An orgasm tore through his body, rocking his world. He locked his knees against the sensation. Waves of pleasure continued rolling down his spine, making him weak. In the midst of his release, he seized Terry's mouth, frantic to taste his tongue. Terry possessed the ability to leave him desperate, frenzied...feverish. Nobody got to him the way this man did. There weren't enough hours in the day, too few minutes. He wanted every single breath leaving the man's lips to belong to him. Owning him wouldn't be enough. Terry made him half-insane. Nothing else could describe the emotions he evoked.

"We need to get out of here," Terry said as soon as Brian gave him enough room to do so. "To my bed, preferably," he added.

"Agreed," Brian said, surprised at how ragged his voice sounded. "We have some time to make up for."

Chapter Five

Straightening out the weights and ensuring each one was in its proper place at No Rival was part of his job. The guys at No Rival were notorious for never putting anything back in the right spot. It was job security, Brian reminded himself for the thousandth time as he made sure each one lined up perfectly. But the chore would never be the same after last night. The weight bench in Terry's basement would never be the same again. A smile pulled at the corners of Brian's mouth at the thought. From now on, he expected he wouldn't be able to set eyes on that particular piece of exercise equipment without getting hard.

An image of Terry's determined expression as he'd urged Brian toward the bench, flashed across his mind, reminding

Brian of the biggest reason why he couldn't get enough. With one look, Terry could make him feel as if he was the only man in the world. It was addictive. The past six weeks with Terry had been like something out of a dream. Even when they were apart, Terry was right there at the forefront of all of his thoughts. A warm weight landed on Brian's shoulder, pulling him from his daydream. Drew was staring at him with raised eyebrows.

"I said your name three times."

Brian hadn't heard a thing. "Sorry. I was..." He didn't know how to finish that sentence.

"Working," Drew supplied, taking mercy on him.

"Sure," Brian agreed thankful for any excuse other than the truth. "Did you need something?"

Drew nodded. "Can I see you in my

office for a minute?" He didn't wait for an answer before heading in that direction. Brian's mind raced as he silently followed. He couldn't think of anything he'd done wrong. Even though Brian had seen Drew chatting endlessly with Rhys, he rarely spoke to Brian. It wasn't that he was unfriendly, merely professional. If Brian was being honest, he didn't tend to invite conversation with anyone at No Rival on a regular basis so Drew wasn't much of an exception.

As Brian claimed the seat on the opposite side of the desk, Drew leaned back in his chair and linked his fingers behind his head. Brian held his silence, doing his best to keep his expression blank as Drew assessed him with his eyes.

"You've been winning a lot of matches lately." Brian nodded even though it had been a rhetorical question.

"I know at one time, you'd hoped to go after the middleweight title. Do you have your sights set on it again?"

It was the moment he'd been dreading. No Rival acted as the current champion's sponsor, leaving Brian unsure of what Drew's reaction would be to one of his employees attempting to dethrone him. Shoring up his courage, Brian nodded. "Looks that way."

Drew spent a moment eyeing him as if attempting to judge how serious he was about the matter. "You do realize Rhys spent months on the road, touring until he earned the right to challenge Terry for the spot, right?"

"I'm aware."

At his answer, Drew sat forward. "All right then. I've drawn up a game plan for you. This is a list of more experienced fighters who are closer to being able to issue a challenge than you are at the moment." He moved some papers around. "There's also a list of venues around the country where matches are being held over the next four months. It's easier to balance training and competing if you fly into the town where the bout is scheduled, train locally and then fly to the next stop the day after each one."

As Drew continued laying out the plans for Brian, he sat in a stunned silence. There was no way he could have done all this research on his own. He never expected Drew would set things up for him. Swallowing down his surprise, Brian forced himself to pay attention.

"What I'm talking about here is an exhausting, grueling schedule. It's not for the faint of heart, but if you're serious, then this is the way. Local bouts are awesome for local exposure, but that's all."

"I understand," Brian said, feeling numb.

"Okay. You should take this shit home and maybe talk it over with Terry since he's your trainer, before making a final decision." At the mention of Terry's name, Brian recognized the biggest flaw in his grand plan. He'd be leaving him behind. His excitement warred with his disappointment. In the end, he knew Terry would expect him to go. He couldn't believe it. Everything he'd dreamed of having was within reach.

* * * * *

Since Brian wasn't an overly talkative person by nature, it took Terry all of two minutes after picking him up to realize he was bursting with enthusiasm. It was either that or he'd gone on a caffeine binge. He was certain the man had recited every detail of his day, including the parts where Terry had been present. By the time he finally got down to the reason for the exhilaration, Terry was ready to set a block on his head to keep him for levitating out of his seat. He was definitely searching his mind for the location of a sturdy roll of duct tape. Having tuned Brian out a bit, it took him a minute to realize he was explaining a countrywide schedule of matches Drew had arranged.

"Drew says if I can survive the four month tour with a seventy-five percent win ratio then I can challenge Rhys for the title."

Brian's hands moved in quick motions as he spoke, proving how excited he was by the prospect. This was what he wanted, Terry reminded himself, keeping his smile in place.

"That's really amazing. You're going straight to the top," Terry assured him. He switched lanes, turning right on Freeman Avenue and in the opposite direction of Warehouse District. "When do you plan to accept?"

The air seemed to change in the truck and Brian fell silent for a moment before answering. "There's more to it than I realized. I have an apartment and bills. I mean, I don't even know what I would do with my car while I was gone." Out of the corner of his eye, Terry saw him shrug. "It's a lot to think about."

He couldn't believe what he was hearing. "You can't be serious. This is what you've been working toward."

Brian groaned. "I know, but I have to be realistic."

"How long do you have until the first fight?"

"Two weeks," Brian answered, sounding disheartened.

Terry tapped his fingers on the steering wheel, turning the problem over in his mind. He couldn't believe Brian would consider turning down such an offer. It wasn't happening. This was what Brian wanted and he would get it. "Let the apartment go," he said, coming to a decision. "There's enough room in my garage for another car and I'm sure we find a spot for the rest of your things at my place."

"I can't ask you do that."

Terry pointed out the obvious. "You didn't."

"Still," Brian said, sounding unsure.

He was blown away that Brian was still arguing. "Do you want this?"

"You know I do."

"Then what'll it hurt? Think about it. If the shoe was on the other foot, would you do the same for me?"

121

Brian didn't hesitate. "Absolutely."

"Then I don't understand the problem."

Brian sputtered for a moment, obviously searching for a loophole. "You asked me to switch places with you. Now, it's your turn. If it was you, would you accept this offer?"

"Absolutely," Terry answered without an ounce of hesitation. "I'd have you right where I want you. Once I was in your house, you'd never get rid of me." He glanced over tossing Brian a wink.

A bark of laughter escaped Brian. "You drive me insane."

Terry smiled at the confession. "Good."

"You're also amazing. Have I told you that lately?"

At Brian's words, Terry knew he'd won. "I don't know, but you will," he promised.

"Promises. Promises," Brian grumbled. "Where are we going anyhow?"

With his eyes focused on the road, Terry smiled. Brian had been so busy talking, it had taken him forever to notice they weren't heading in the direction of their usual Friday night destination. "You're finally getting everything you deserve. I think this calls for a celebration."

Brian groaned. "No alcohol." His plea surprised a chuckle from Terry. "No alcohol," he promised. "I have something better in mind."

"That's a broad statement. There's a thousand things I'd rather be doing."

Thinking it over, Terry conceded the point. "True, but there's only one or two things better than cheesecake."

* * * * *

Thankfully, Terry's cheesecake place turned out to be some tiny off-the-beaten-path place with a drive-thru. He'd ordered for them both. Brian hadn't paid much attention to what he'd gotten him. The only thought rolling through his mind was they'd soon be home. With the takeout boxes sitting between them, they spent the remainder of the drive to Terry's house in silence. The man had done so much for him. Brian didn't know how to begin repaying him. There wasn't a single thing he could think to say that would cover how he felt. The day he'd met Terry, the universe had blessed him with more than a friend, mentor and lover. He'd been given the world.

Brian chose a spot on the couch as Terry went in search of forks and drinks. Sinking down into the plush, light-brown leather, Brian's nerve endings danced with the need to act. The more he thought about everything Terry had given him, the more he wanted to do something insane, like scream at the top of his lungs how wonderful Terry was until he lost his voice. It was crazy but at least it would be something. Right now, he felt as if he contributed nothing to their relationship. They were uneven. Terry's every action showed his love. Brian was just there.

By the time Terry reappeared, Brian was ready to jump out of his skin. The moment their gazes met, Terry's brows drew together in confusion making Brian wonder what he'd seen in his face.

"Come here," Brian demanded. At the husky note in his voice, Terry's expression cleared. Dumping the items he'd gone in search of on the coffee table, Terry did as Brian bade, coming to stand over him. The moment he was within reach, Brian hooked the belt loop of Terry's jeans with his forefinger tugging while patting his knee.

"Sit." At his command, Terry's eyebrows rose in challenge. Brian softened his tone. "I want to hold you." Terry obeyed. They were both too tall for this sort of shit but Brian didn't give a fuck. As soon as he had Terry in his lap, he pressed the button next to him, releasing the footrest. The backward momentum combined with Brian's grip at his waist left Terry little choice except to relax his spine against Brian's chest. Obviously accepting his fate, Terry settled in, allowing Brian's groin to cradle his ass and resting his head on Brian's shoulder. Brian tightened his arms around Terry's waist, burying his hands beneath his shirt until he held on to bare skin.

"Much better," he sighed against

Terry's ear. Every doubt he had over his ability to hang onto such a beautiful man melted away once he held him in his embrace.

"You gonna tell me what's wrong?"

Feeling too insecure to admit to being insecure, Brian chose another truth instead. "Sometimes being close to you isn't close enough, you know?"

Terry ran his hands over Brian's forearms. "Yeah, I get that." An unexpected grin touched Brian's lips. It came from the inside out. Terry's tone made Brian realize Terry truly did understand. He hadn't been so happy in a long time. Holding Terry was almost surreal. The warmth of his body seeped into Brian's skin. Before he realized what he was doing, he was rubbing small circles on Terry's stomach. Terry's breathing hitched up a notch and Brian went hard at the sound. Chill bumps rose beneath Brian's fingertips. He touched his lips to the side of Terry's neck.

"How am I supposed to go four months without you?"

"You'll be too busy to think of me," Terry said, sounding more than turned on and sexy as hell. Taking advantage, Brian worked the button of Terry's jeans loose and slid the zipper down. He went slow, partially in an attempt to draw out the anticipation but he also wanted to torture Terry a little to get even for the remark. As if he could ever be too busy to think of him.

Freeing Terry's erection, Brian drew a steadying breath. This wasn't about him. He needed to show this man how he felt. It wasn't enough to love him. It would never be enough. He wanted to set the world at his feet. Brian wrapped his fingers around Terry's cock. A moan vibrated from his body. He stroked him, handling his dick the way he would his own. Terry moved against his hand, keeping pace. Brian swore the pleasure was his. The ass grinding against his erection nearly had him coming in his jeans. Every muscle in Terry's body tensed. Brian buried his face against his shoulder, biting Terry's shirt in a vain attempt at hanging onto his sanity as Terry's orgasm hit and Brian's name fell from his lips. When his heart couldn't stand it any longer, he turned his head, pressing his face against Terry's neck and breathing in his scent. When it still wasn't enough, he opened his mouth over the column of his neck, brushing his tongue along the cord. Terry made a move as if to pull away, but Brian held him in place.

"If you're keeping me here then I

can't do all the things to you I'm picturing in my head." The teasing note in Terry's voice caused Brian to chuckle. However, he still wasn't ready to let him go.

"Hush and let me play."

Terry relaxed again. "Whatever you say."

"Mmm, I do like the sound of that."

"I do feel moved to point out my shirt is a bit uncomfortably wet."

At the complaint, Brian snagged the hem and carefully pulled it over Terry's head, trying to keep from making the mess worse. The moment he had Terry divested of the material, he cupped Terry's jaw and tilted his head back, capturing his mouth with his own. When their tongues met, Brian's heart slammed against his chest. This man would never understand. He loved him so goddamn much. It was killing him.

Chapter Six

A warm tingle landed between his shoulder blades, luring Terry away from his dreams. A smile grew from the inside out at the sensation of Brian's lips trailing down his spine. In spite of his exhaustion, he arched into the touch.

"Someone's being lazy this morning."

Keeping his eyes closed and gripping the pillow tighter, Terry chuckled. "I'm entitled."

Brian hummed against his skin. "You're something. I'll give you that."

Terry laughed harder, but didn't budge. With a huff, Brian settled in next to him, tugging him back against his chest. Terry didn't protest. He'd almost dozed off again when Brian spoke against his ear.

"I can't believe you're not dragging me out of bed by the ankle, forcing me to go to the gym."

Lifting his head, Terry opened one eye and peeked at the clock. "You have to work this afternoon and I'm going with McKenna to her doctor's appointment today."

Brian kissed the side of his neck. His hand skimmed down Terry's side, over his hip. Terry held his breath as he focused on the motion. "I have you all to myself for a little while longer then. How should we pass the time?" Freezing an inch away from Terry's twitching cock, Brian touched his lips the shell of his ear. Each breath the man drew caused a new wave of chills to race over Terry's skin. With his concentration locked on the things Brian did to his body, Terry forgot to answer. Brian sighed.

"You never sleep in. I guess I should leave you to it." The hard dick against Terry's ass told a different story. Pressing closer, Terry swallowed a laugh when Brian started panting.

"I guess so."

When cool air touched his back, Terry bit back an irritated groan. He shouldn't have been surprised Brian had taken him seriously. It wasn't as if the man couldn't tell he was aroused, but he was too much of a gentleman to press. If he weren't so tired, he'd chase Brian down. As it was, he couldn't peel his lids open long enough to figure out where he'd run off to. Of course, now he was too turned on to go back to sleep. Kicking the covers away, he decided he could force his eyes open for this. It lasted half a second before he found his face pressed against the pillow. Brian covered his body with his.

"Where do you think you're going?"

"Wherever you are."

"Damn right," Brian growled as he sank his teeth into Terry's shoulder. "I still have to get my daily exercise." He'd gone to put on a condom, Terry realized as Brian burrowed his hand between Terry's body and the mattress, fisting Terry's cock. It didn't matter that Brian didn't have much room to maneuver. Terry found himself moaning and moving against Brian's palm in a matter of moments. Damn. The man had a way of keeping him on the edge of explosion. Shifting positions, he kneed Terry's legs apart, settling in between them. The ease in which he pushed inside told Terry some lubrication had gone on as well while he'd been missing. Once fully seated, Brian held still.

Terry wanted more. "You're killing me."

"I'm trying to make it last. You feel too damn good and I never want it to end." Brian's admission stole Terry's breath away. He always said the right things. Of course, it didn't dampen his need. "Fuck me."

As the plea left his lips, Brian's control seemed to snap. Pulling out slightly, he slammed home again. Terry moved against the palm still gripping his cock. His mind became a haze of pleasurable sensations between tugging on his dick and the way Brian hit all the right places internally.

Burying his face into the pillow, he held his breath, clamping his back teeth tight as an orgasm shot through him. The sound of Brian's harsh cursing barely penetrated his high. The sheet clung to his skin from the evidence of his ecstasy. He didn't care. His heart was near to bursting. Brian's lips touched his shoulder. He couldn't move.

"You're so fucking sexy when you come," Brian said as he rolled to his side, giving Terry room to breathe. Not that he wanted it. Oxygen wasn't nearly as important to him as Brian. Turning his head, he brought the man into focus. A thin layer of sweat coated Brian's face. With his eyes closed, he visibly struggled to regain his breath. Terry's heart swelled at the sight. In that moment, he wished for a different life. A longer one.

"Brian." The word left his lips so quietly Terry didn't think he would hear it. One eye popped open, proving him wrong.

"Are you okay?"

"Yeah." Terry wanted to tell him everything, his reasons for retiring and about the sheer terror choking him. He needed him to know everything that was slowly dragging him under but he couldn't do it. Instead, he said the only thing that truly mattered. "I love you." Brian's brow furrowed. There was no way he'd missed the sad note to Terry's words. "I don't want to move," Terry added before Brian could question him.

His expression cleared. A tiny grin hovered on his lips. "I guess you need a shower before McKenna gets here." Terry closed his eyes, pretending to cry. Brian snorted before quickly kissing him. "Come on, lazy ass," he said, pulling Terry from the bed. "You need to get ready."

As soon as Terry was on his feet, Brian hauled him against his chest, leaving no room between them. Touching his lips to Terry's, his tongue brushed the corner of his mouth. The moment Terry

137

opened for him, Brian held nothing back, devouring him. By the time Brian pulled away, Terry was ready to go again. Resting his forehead against Terry's, Brian's eyelashes fluttered against his cheeks as if he fought to control his body. Terry watched him in silence, wishing he could cling to him forever.

"By the way," Brian said, sounding every bit as desperate as Terry felt. "I love you too."

* * * * *

"I forgot to ask where you told Brian you were going today."

"I said you had a doctor's appointment."

McKenna nodded as she snapped her seatbelt in place. "He didn't wonder why Kurt wasn't going with me?"

"I'm sure he did," Terry admitted as he turned to stare out the passenger side window. "But I reminded him before you got there that Kurt is going to morning PTSD therapy sessions now."

McKenna put the car in drive. "You'll have to tell him eventually."

Keeping his eyes locked on the passing scenery, Terry didn't hesitate before lying his ass off. "I will." Thankfully, McKenna didn't call him on it. He didn't have the brain power to deal with it at that moment. The truth was, he didn't know what to do. Brian could break out, surging to the top any day now. Terry didn't have the heart to ruin his dreams. His throat swelled and he swallowed against the sensation. Life was so cruel. Even though he'd wanted to own Brian from the first moment they met, he'd tried to keep their relationship from progressing to this point. At any time before Brian's first fight, he could've put a stop to it. After that night together, he'd lost the will. More importantly, he'd lost his heart.

"What's Brian up to today?" McKenna asked, as if she knew where his head had gone.

"He's at No Rival, working his final shift." He still couldn't look at her.

"Would you like me to take you there instead of back to your house?" Before he could ask why, she added, "I don't think you should be alone with your thoughts right now. Between going to lunch, the doctor and getting your head shaved, I think we've killed all the time we can without you crashing out on me."

Terry snorted. "I'll be fine." As if his body decided to make a liar out of him, a sharp pain sliced through his chest and a wave of exhaustion washed over him.

"Your hair looks great," McKenna said, reaching over and running her hand over the short stubble. It was obvious she was attempting to distract him. "Brian will love it. It's so soft."

He closed his eyes. The thought of Brian made him smile in spite of everything horrible going on his life. "Yeah. You can drop me by No Rival and thanks for going with me today," he said, without opening his eyes. Although it seemed as if only a few seconds passed, when McKenna touched his arm, he blinked in confusion at the sight of No Rival's nondescript steel door.

"Are you okay?"

The look of concern on McKenna's face reminded him why he didn't want to tell Brian. He wouldn't be able to stand having Brian look at him the way she was right now.

"Yeah. I'm good." Without giving McKenna a chance to pull away, Terry set his hand over hers. Holding her in place, he met her gaze. "I'm sorry."

Her brow furrowed. "Why?"

"I hate that I'm forcing you to hide things from your friend."

A smile lit her face. In true McKenna style, she didn't see things the same as everyone else did. "Lucky for you, I lie for a living." He shook his head. His brother had been the luckiest bastard alive to have her on his side. "Time to put your brave face on," she ordered. "If you plan to keep this hidden from Brian, you need to smirk a little more."

Rolling his eyes, Terry shoved open his car door. Only McKenna would give someone tips on how best to get away with keeping secrets. At the doorway, Terry punched in the security code he'd been given back when he'd still been a member. He half-expected it wouldn't work and was little more than surprised when the light flashed green, allowing them slip inside the private club.

Drew Alexander, the U.S. Heavyweight Champion and owner of No Rival, glanced up from his desk as they stepped through the door. At six-foot-four and two hundred and thirty-five pounds, the huge male cleared a path everywhere he went. He stood, meeting them halfway. The light glimmered off his baldhead. In spite of his intimidating appearance, Drew was a good person. Terry would go so far as to say he was one of the best people he knew. Drew spent more time raising money for different charitable projects than he did training for bouts. McKenna eyed the man as if taking his measurements for her next book.

"Terry," Drew called, a luminous smile stretching across his face. "Long time, no see. Who's your friend?"

Terry touched McKenna's elbow, urging her forward. "This is McKenna Travis."

"Ah. Kurt's wife. Your infamy precedes you." She liked that. It was written all over her face. Terry almost snorted at the mischievous glint lighting her eyes. "I'm Drew," he added before Terry could introduce him.

"Can I touch your head?"

It took every ounce of Terry's self-control to keep from laughing when Drew immediately leaned over, allowing her to run her hand over his head. No matter how hard he tried, he couldn't hide the humor in his tone. "This is hardly the first time you've met a bald man. Gray was bald for a long time before he died."

She rubbed his head one more time as if memorizing the texture. "Yes, but he lost his hair during chemo. I was curious to know if it felt different shaved."

"Brian shaves his head," Terry pointed out. "You could've asked him at any time." A small smile played on her lips. "I know."

Bent at the waist and staring at the floor, Drew broke in. "Mrs. Travis, as the owner of this establishment, I feel moved to point out if someone drops a weight, you'll lose a toe." Terry looked down. Her feet were bare.

Tilting his head to one side, Terry tried to remember if she'd been wearing anything on them earlier. Surely he would've noticed something like that. "Where are your shoes?"

McKenna's face went blank. She dropped her hand. "Why would anyone hold a weight over my foot?" Drew watched her in silence. Terry didn't doubt he was searching his mind for a counterargument. She wasn't finished. "Even if we put aside the fact it would be barbaric for anyone to attempt to squash a pregnant lady's toes, I can't get around my stomach to tie my shoes. Therefore, I have to assume it would take a great deal of effort for someone to position themselves where such a thing was possible. Since I'm not blind nor am I simpleton, wouldn't this then allow me enough time to simply step aside?"

It was a nervous tic. McKenna reacted one of two ways to every situation—with excessive sexual innuendo or heightened intelligence. No matter which way she swung, people were helpless against her and Terry could see Drew was no exception. He was visibly fighting against a smile while she seemed to be waiting for him to prove her wrong.

When Drew took a moment too long to respond she let out a heavy sigh. "I release you of all legal ramifications. Is that better?"

A low chuckle fell from his lips. "Damn. Where's that fancy lawyer who's always hanging around here when I need him?"

"I take it back," she said immediately. "In hindsight I can see how Asher would be capable of distracting me with his beauty long enough to drop a weight on me should he decide to try."

This time, Terry couldn't hide his reaction to Drew's expression. It was obvious he had no idea what to make of her. "You knew who I was talking about with only the description of 'fancy lawyer' to go by?"

"I had coffee with him this morning."

"What does that have to with

anything?"

McKenna didn't miss a beat. "He looked every bit as yummy as ever in his expensive business suit."

Drew being outrageous in his own right, chose a different track. "I thought coffee was bad for pregnant women."

McKenna shrugged. "How should I know? I don't drink the stuff."

Terry thought Drew's eyes might have crossed, but it passed quickly. "Damn. I'd love to have been a fly on the wall when Kurt met you."

Terry had the exact same reaction when he'd learned the pair were dating. If there was anyone who did a better job at keeping people off balance than McKenna, it was her husband Kurt. His intelligence left everyone he met in awe.

"He called me crazy then handcuffed me to his bed."

Drew threw his head back on a roar of laughter, drawing the gaze of several of the club's patrons. At the commotion, Brian appeared from around the corner. A smile lit his face at the sight of them. Every single one of Terry's nerve ending fired to life. Being near Brian was the same as a shot adrenaline to the heart.

"I thought I heard your voice."

Before Terry had a chance to make an ass of himself by hauling Brian against him, McKenna released a loud huff, snagging his attention. "Brian isn't wearing shoes either!"

This time it was Drew with the blank expression. "What's your point?"

Terry could've interceded by letting her know they weren't allowed to have them on while sparring, but he secretly thought she was merely fucking with Drew. She narrowed her eyes at the man.

"You're a bad one. I like it."

While the pair were distracted, Terry gave Brian a tiny shove in the direction of the locker room. Taking the hint, Brian stepped to the side and slipped inside. After a quick glance around, ensuring they were alone, Terry tugged him closer. He loved the happiness written on Brian's face. No one was ever excited to see him. It was obvious Brian was now.

"You cut off all your hair. How did McKenna's appoint—"

Terry sealed his mouth over Brian's before he was forced to lie to the man about anything. He spoke against Brian's lips. "Couldn't wait to see you."

"Missed you," Brian agreed. Terry's shirt stretched across his back as Brian tightened his hold on the material. A throat cleared to their left. Even though it was ridiculous—since they were in a public place—Terry turned his head ready to blast whoever was interrupting them. He didn't release Brian.

With one shoulder leaning against the doorframe, Drew stood with his arms crossed over his chest, eyeing them curiously. "I assume you're renewing your membership with me now."

He could feel Brian shaking with suppressed laughter. Terry cleared his throat. "Um. Yeah. I guess I need to do that while I'm here."

With a sharp nod, Drew pushed away from the wall. "Nobody fucking works around here." Brian shook harder as Drew somehow managed to make the words sound as if he was the most put upon man in the world.

"Yeah, about that," Terry said apologetically. "Brian needs to leave early." Drew let a colorful curse fly as he left them alone. The moment he was gone, Terry finally looked at Brian. His eyes shone with mirth. "I think that went well."

"Since today was my last day, it's not as if he could fire me for messing around while on the clock or anything," Brian pointed out reasonably. His expression sobered as his hold tightened on Terry's shirt. "As for all of this," he said, tugging him flush against his body. "I'm damn proud to call you mine. Sorry if you hoped to keep me a secret because I don't work that way."

It hadn't occurred to Terry that it would be an issue. "The idea never even crossed my mind. I couldn't hide the way I feel about you even I wanted to." He stared at Brian's mouth for a moment longer, gathering his strength. "Get dressed. This is our last night for a while." He stepped away. "I'll go pay Drew's astronomical membership fee and make him smile again. If I stay in here with you, we both know I won't keep my hands to myself."

"Later."

Recognizing the promise in Brian's tone, Terry dipped his chin in agreement. "Later."

*

Brian rushed through ripping off his grappling tape before hauling on his street clothes. He need not have hurried. With his gym bag in hand, he found Terry, McKenna, Drew and Asher—who seemed to have magically appeared while he'd been changing clothes—sequestered in Drew's office with their heads together, quietly discussing something. Asher was the first to notice him hovering in the doorway and he tossed Brian a wink. Since they didn't appear finished with whatever they were discussing, Brian leaned his shoulder into the doorframe, prepared to wait.

The Italian lawyer, Asher D'Ettore, was at No Rival almost as often as Brian was. His jet-black hair coupled with light-blue eyes made him stand out in any crowd even without taking his more-expensive-than-Brian's-car business suit and amazing accent into account. He had McKenna tucked under one arm and from Brian's vantage point, it looked as if she was sniffing him while attempting to appear as if she wasn't. Since the first moment they'd been introduced, McKenna had made no secret of her love for all things Asher. Brian felt sure if there wasn't a list of things standing between them, she'd be climbing the man like a monkey. Of course, that list did exist. It began with McKenna's husband, Kurt and ended with Asher's husband, Rhys. As if the thought conjured him, Rhys appeared at his side in the doorway.

"Did I miss a meeting?"

Brian glanced over at the man who currently held the title he intended to steal and lifted his shoulder. "I have no idea. If so, then I missed the memo as well."

"Huh," Rhys grunted absently, before adding, "Damn. McKenna is trying to steal my man again. I can't turn my back for a minute." His words so closely mimicked Brian's thoughts, he couldn't help but laugh. A wicked smile touched Rhys' lips at the sound. If there was anyone who equaled Asher in heart-stopping beauty, it was Rhys D'Ettore. He was a lethal combination of sexy and charming. Everyone smiled while in his presence and Brian genuinely liked him. It wouldn't stop him from challenging him, but still.

"I'm being serious," Rhys added. His tone couldn't have possibly sounded less than he claimed. "Neither pregnancy nor getting married to Kurt has slowed down her pursuit. If I don't step up my game, she'll whip some freaky move out of one of her erotica novels and I'll never see my husband again. Look at that bag she's carrying, I guarantee she has at least one pair of handcuffs inside."

The further Rhys took his rant, the harder Brian laughed. It wasn't a good move since Rhys was the type of outrageous a person shouldn't feed. He would only get worse, but Brian couldn't help it. Plus, now that Rhys mentioned it, Brian couldn't stop eyeing McKenna's purse. He didn't doubt for one minute she did have handcuffs inside. Their antics seemed to penetrate the group surrounding Drew's desk. Terry turned in their direction, scowling.

"Quit flirting with Brian, Rhys. He's mine." At Terry's growled statement, Brian's cheeks ached as his smile stretched even wider. Undeterred, Rhys' brown eyes flashed with good humor. He threw his arms wide, and pitched his voice loud enough that Brian felt sure everyone inside the club could hear him.

"But we're bored. We don't like to be left out."

Terry shook his head and tossed a glance in Asher's direction. "How do you stand it? He's like a child."

A slow grin spread across Asher's face, but he didn't respond. Rhys answered for him. "He happens to think I'm wonderful. Don't you babe? Tell him you think I'm awesome."

"He is indeed awesome," Asher

answered dutifully. Brian didn't miss the honesty behind the statement. They might have been playing, but Asher truly meant it. Drew was pretending to beat his head on the desk.

"Why? Why do I pretend things will get done around here? I should close up shop and become a stay-at-home dad."

Even though Brian could hear the humor in Drew's voice, he immediately felt guilty. Drew did a lot for other people and he was more than tolerant of their antics around the club. Actually, if he didn't qualify for sainthood, Brian didn't know who did.

"Sorry," he mumbled, attempting to school his features into some semblance of seriousness. "Carry on with whatever."

Terry's expression hardened. Brian could tell Terry didn't like him apologizing to anyone but he kept his mouth shut.

Manners mattered to Brian and Terry knew it.

Drew sat up and waved them inside. "No. The two of you should be in on this since we're plotting on your behalf."

Brian listened in with equal parts horror and respect for their devious minds as Drew and Terry took turns explaining how they saw the future unfolding. It seemed they already knew exactly how to keep Rhys a champion and make Brian into one while all the way making No Rival into the ultimate place to learn how become a top contender.

With his mind still racing from all the new information he'd been fed, Brian drove home, barely noticing the silence in the car. Terry was even less talkative than usual. By the time Brian stepped beneath the pounding hot water in the shower, he'd come to some type of grips with the secret Rhys and Drew had been keeping until now. Rhys had his eye on the light heavyweight title. It was easy enough to achieve the weight class. He did sit right on the line with his size. It could be done. Forcibly, Brian pushed thoughts of his future aside. The minor tweak in Drew's plans meant Brian wouldn't need to be gone quite as long as he'd originally thought, but it was still a long tour. It was still his last night with Terry. Once that knowledge settled on his shoulders again, he couldn't concentrate on anything else. Man he hoped he didn't fuck up their relationship by going on this tour. He did not want to trade one thing for the other. As much as he'd always dreamed of becoming a champion, he already held the world.

Terry's silence nagged at the back of his mind. This path was every bit as much

Terry's doing as it was Brian's desire. Therefore, he knew he wasn't upset with him for leaving. It was something else. He couldn't put his finger on it. He made it through his shower by simply going through the motions. With his mind focused on the problem, he wrapped a towel around his waist, dismissing the drops of water still rolling down his body. Inside the closet, he stood with his hands on his hips and stared at nothing. It seemed so odd to have his clothes hanging alongside Terry's.

"How long do you intend to hide in here?"

Brian looked over in surprise at Terry's question. He was relaxing against the doorframe as if he'd been there awhile. His light-blue dress shirt was unbuttoned and hanging open, showing off his delicious torso.

"You never said what we were doing tonight. I couldn't decide what I needed to wear." It was only half a lie. Terry hadn't ever said what they were doing.

"I'm all about you. Whatever you want works for me. If you want to make the rounds and tell everyone goodbye, we will. If you'd rather go to dinner, we'll do that instead."

"I could eat."

Terry straightened away from the doorway. "Then that's what we'll do," he said, as he moved to button his shirt. Suddenly, whatever was going on became too much. Terry's mood seemed strained and Brian hated it. Without thought, Brian snagged the lapels of Terry's shirt before he could get the first button done. He hauled the man against him.

"I'm starving, but I didn't say a goddamn word about going anywhere." He slammed his mouth down on Terry's with enough force that their teeth bumped.

Dragging the shirt halfway down Terry's arms, Brian kept him trapped as he walked him backward toward the bed while continuing to eat at Terry's mouth. Terry willingly submitted to Brian's demands. Brian didn't doubt for a second that Terry could overpower him if he chose to do so. The hitch in Terry's breathing said more than anything else could have as the back of his knees hit the edge of the bed. It was obvious Terry was enjoying the loss of control. With a push, Brian urged Terry onto his back before straddling his hips. He couldn't get enough of tasting the man's lips. Without showing an ounce of mercy, Brian used his teeth, tongue and strength to tease his mouth. When Terry struggled free of his shirtsleeves and gripped the back of Brian's neck, he moved his lips to Terry's throat, sucking lightly at the skin there.

"I don't like your distance," Brian confessed against his skin. "You're not allowed to put space here," he added, as he moved to Terry's collarbone. Terry cupped his jaw, urging Brian to meet his gaze.

"Nothing gets between us, okay? Nothing," Terry stressed, making Brian wonder who he was trying to convince. "Going to that appointment today with McKenna, it's got my head in a dark place, thinking about death and shit. I shouldn't have let it ruin our time together." Brian got it and it should've occurred to him sooner. As excited as Terry's was about McKenna's baby, she was still his brother's widow. Gray's death had to have been sitting on his chest the whole time he'd been at the doctor with her.

"You don't have to do anything alone," Brian reminded him. A mischievous grin touched Terry's lips. He rolled his hips, reminding Brian of every spot their bodies touched.

"For the next few months, I'll be handling quite a few things alone."

"You'd fucking better," Brian growled before he could stop himself. The thought of anyone else touching Terry made him want to kill someone. Terry's hands moved to his shoulders before traveling down his chest and ribs until he reached the edge of Brian's towel.

"You've got a jealous streak I would've never suspected. I like it."

Brian didn't. "It's new to me. No one else has ever brought it out and I can't say I care for the feeling." The towel slipped away from his hips. Brian allowed his gaze to slide over Terry's features, taking in every detail. He zeroed in on his mouth. With his focus locked on Terry's bottom lip, he touched his thumb to it and stroked it lightly. "I love the sexy new haircut, by the way."

Terry chuckled at the remark. "Does my mouth remind you of my hair?"

Shifting his gaze back to Terry's, Brian didn't share in his humor. "I was reminded I don't tell you often enough how sexy you are." Brian dipped his head, pausing right before meeting Terry's lips. "You'll scream my name," he promised before capturing Terry's mouth. The man's flavor and the scent of his cologne teased Brian's senses, turning him on even more. As the first moan vibrated from the back of Terry's throat, Brian experienced a never-seen-before level of determination. His promise wouldn't be merely a boast. Before he left in the morning, Terry would scream his name.

Chapter Seven

August

"How did it go today?"

"I sat around for hours waiting for my match to start. You know how it is, boring as hell."

Terry blew out a sigh. "You know what I mean. Did you win?"

"Yep."

"Hell yeah!" Terry cheered. "Of course you did because you're fucking awesome." Even though Terry couldn't see him, Brian still blushed. He'd always been uncomfortable with praise.

"What did you do today?"

Terry laughed knowingly at the change of topic. "Fine. We'll talk about something else. I went to see Drew in hopes he'd be interested in helping me put together some type of fundraiser for Betty.

Anna's long illness and death left her with a mountain of bills. Buying flowers won't cut it any longer. She'll have to accept help whether she wants it or not."

Damn. He loved this man. "Is he going to help?"

"Yeah. We kicked around a few ideas. It'll take some work, but it's not like I have anything else occupying my time."

Feeling wicked, Brian pitched his voice low. "Do you need something to keep your hands busy?"

"You sound as if you have something in mind."

"Always."

There was shuffling in the background as if Terry was settling in. "I'm your one-man captive audience."

Brian set his elbows on the bar and leaned his shoulder against the wall, thankful he'd chosen the quiet, darkened corner to make this call. "Where are you right now?"

"Kicked back on the couch."

His eyes fell closed and he drew a slow breath in through his nose before opening his eyes again. "I do love that couch. Are you sitting in my spot?" He knew Terry would know exactly the location he referred. The place where he'd held Terry in his arms while stroking his cock would always be his.

"I am."

"Damn," Brian sighed. "I wish I was there with you. I can practically taste the back of your neck right now."

Terry made a noise between a moan and sigh. "Of all the things you've tasted, that's the one that comes to mind?"

"Oh yeah, the back of your neck is awesome. As soon as my lips touch it, chill bumps cover your skin and you go hard for me. Not only is it sexy as hell, it does something to my chest."

"Where are you right now?"

"The hotel bar."

"Go to your room," Terry demanded. The husky order caused a low chuckle to slip past Brian's lips.

"Why should I?"

His question met a long pause before Terry answered. "Look at your phone." Holding it away from him, Brian glanced at the screen. An image of Terry, bare-chested and covered in a flush of arousal met his gaze. A wave of longing washed over him. Reluctantly, he gave up his prize and put the phone back to his ear.

"Goddamn, Terry," he growled.

"I love the sound of my name on your lips. Go to your room," he repeated.

Brian's erection throbbed, making

him almost whimper. "I don't know if I can move."

"I won't wait forever so you'd better get going." At Terry's threat, Brian caught the bartender's attention, making sure the man saw him throw a twenty on the bar before heading for the elevator. It dinged loudly as the doors slid open.

"Are you going?"

"For fuck's sake, Terry, you're killing me?"

A red-haired woman Brian recognized as the girlfriend of one of the other fighters, smiled brightly at him making him realize he wasn't alone. She stepped aside, giving him room to step inside the elevator. He almost groaned. Terry had him so tied up in knots he hadn't noticed her presence. Blushing again, he stared at the opposite wall after pushing the button for his floor.

"For fuck's sake isn't an answer," Terry said silkily. The words caressed Brian's ear, going straight to his already leaking cock, making him twitch.

"Heading that way," Brian said, hoping the woman couldn't hear the lust in his voice. As things were, if she looked down she'd lose an eye.

"Good. You'll want to be alone when I tell you all about how I want to take you to the back of my throat."

Brian tilted his head back and focused on the ceiling. He wasn't sure if he was seeking guidance, praying for strength or hoping the poor woman stuck in the otherwise quiet space couldn't hear Terry's words.

"Of course, that's after I tongue your slit, swiping away the delicious pre-cum."

The door slid open, releasing Brian from his prison. "You're fucking evil,"

Brian growled quietly. The redhead's musical laughter followed him off the elevator. He was beyond caring. Holding the phone trapped between his shoulder and ear, he dug around in his wallet for the keycard to his room. The second the door closed behind him, he tossed everything except the phone to the floor. Without taking another step, he fell back against it and ripped open his jeans.

"Can you feel my throat tightening around your dick yet?" Terry taunted.

"I wouldn't miss a minute of it," Brian answered, never meaning anything more as he palmed his erection.

"Your hand is holding the back of my head as you fuck my mouth." Closing his eyes, Brian pictured Terry's mouth in place of his hand.

"Damn, Brian. I love the sounds you make when you're about to come. I wish I really was there sucking you off."

"Want you here. Want to be inside you," Brian admitted, barely able to think. The hitch in Terry's breathing came through the line loud and clear. The sound sent him over the edge. Hot semen rolled down his fingers. His knees almost gave out. As the orgasm left him gasping, he chanted the only thing his mind was able to hang onto. "Love you. Love you so much."

For weeks afterward, Brian would murmur those words in the exact same tone on a nightly basis while Terry teased him without mercy. By nine weeks into Brian's tour, he was replaying every single moment of those encounters wondering exactly where everything went wrong.

*

Terry was intentionally avoiding a majority of Brian's calls. It was too hard to stay silent. Things hadn't started out this way, and he wasn't even sure when it truly began. One day the phone rang and Terry couldn't bring himself to answer. As he watched Brian's name flashing on the screen, he knew a moment of weakness. In that span of thirty seconds of paralyzing fear, Terry had wanted Brian with him more than he wanted Brian's dreams to come true. He'd known the truth then. It was time to start letting go.

He'd been forced to promise McKenna the moon to keep her quiet and by moon he meant he'd given his word he'd come clean to Brian on his own. Tonight, he promised himself for the hundredth time. He'd force the words past his throat if it was the last thing he did. Brian deserved so much better than him. He wanted to call him, hear his voice. Every time he dialed his number, he cleared the screen before hitting send. No matter how often he imagined different ways to drop the bomb, he couldn't do it.

Standing on the sidewalk outside G. Richards' Bookstore, Terry let the sun of the day soak into his skin. He'd met with Asher earlier in the day, making sure his shit was in order. After meeting the lawyer for coffee at the bookstore café, he'd hoped for a small sense of peace. There was none. As he stood mere feet from where Gray had taken his own life, his state of mind continued its downward spiral. A wave of exhaustion washed over him. Was he only thirty-five? Damn. He felt at least twice that age. Everything ached, especially his heart. He'd overdone it today but it had been a necessary evil. In a flash, a lead weight landed on his shoulders. It was as if he were dragging himself across broken glass as he made his way to the alleyway where his brother had drawn his last breath. The metal staircase leading to McKenna's apartment above the bookstore came into view and Terry knew he wouldn't make it. He closed his eyes for a moment. When he opened them again, Kurt stood in front of him. Concern etched his every feature.

"Hey man. Are you okay?" Kurt's question sounded as if they were standing in a tunnel. Everything went black.

* * * * *

Sitting at the bar of some hotel in a town he couldn't remember the name of became a nightly routine Brian hated passionately. The food was always overpriced and everything tasted like ash the longer he went without hearing from Terry. Most nights, it seemed as if they were simply on some sort of fucking passing ships schedule. It wasn't as if he had any room to complain. He was chasing his dream. Terry was trying to help someone in need. It didn't change a damn thing. He was still sick of shit being this way. In his heart, he knew he'd expected their relationship to stay the way it had been when he first left, jacking off while talking as dirty as possible into Terry's ear each night. Even though it wasn't realistic to believe it could be that way forever, he still wanted it.

He tried calling one more time. Thankfully, unlike the past six times when it had gone straight to voicemail, it rang.

Terry's voice slurred when he answered. He sounded less than half-awake. Brian thought he heard a beep in the background but it was impossible to tell with the noise of the overcrowded bar drowning everything out.

"Did I wake you?"

"Yeah. It's okay."

Damn. It seemed they were always out of sync. As the silence stretched on, a wave of loneliness swept over him. He could almost picture Terry hovering between awake and asleep. It was one of his favorite times to watch him. His face lost its hard edge. In those unguarded moments, Brian knew Terry was the one for him. Longing crawled up his skin. He wanted to be with him instead of this fucking place.

"Is everything okay?"

A smile touched Brian's lips at the question. Terry knew him too well. "Worn out," he lied, not wanting to sound ungrateful. He knew this is what Terry had worked so hard to help him achieve. Before Terry could question him further, he forced a hint of cheerfulness into his tone. "I guess I should let you get some sleep. It's easy to forget about the time difference."

Terry didn't respond right away. It was almost as if he was trying to decide if he should press. "This is harder than I expected," Terry said, taking him by surprise. Brian's eyes fell closed. A lump formed in his throat. He swallowed against it.

"Yeah." Brian's heart couldn't take any further admissions from Terry. The fact he'd been trying to call for the past two hours while Terry's phone behaved as if it had been turned off had his head reeling now that he knew Terry was in bed. What if he'd been avoiding Brian's call because he hadn't been alone? He couldn't stand the thought. Clearing his throat, Brian did his best to hide the hurt welling inside him.

"I honestly didn't realize the time." It

was a total lie, but he couldn't stop. "I just wanted to hear your voice, but I should let you go back to sleep." His words were met with silence. Fuck. He wanted to put his fist through the wall. He waved for the bartender to bring him another shot.

"I'm sorry."

The quiet apology felt a lot like the final straw to Brian. "Yeah me too." Problem was, he didn't know why. He tossed back the shot and motioned for another. It burned all the way down.

"Brian."

"Yeah."

He didn't say anything more. Brian tossed back another. When he was able to breathe again, he decided he'd tortured them both enough for one night. "Go back to sleep, okay? I'm sorry for calling late."

"All right." At Terry's quiet response,

Brian disconnected the call before he made a fool of himself. Apparently recognizing his desperation, the bartender refilled his shot glass without Brian asking.

"Are you allowed to leave the bottle?"

"Sure thing," he answered, making Brian's night.

"Cool." Brian didn't meet his stare. Instead, he chose to watch the fireworks on the opposite side of the room. The same red-haired woman he'd seen at every match yelled something Brian couldn't make out at the blue-haired fighter she was traveling with. It seemed he wasn't the only one with problems. Taking in the fact she was visibly pregnant, he accepted hers might be worse.

It took him a few minutes to realize the guy working the bar still hadn't moved away. Focusing on him for the first time, Brian raised his eyebrows in question while doing his best to hide his surprise. The guy's hooded gaze did nothing to mask his thoughts. Once he had Brian's attention a lazy smile touched his lips.

"Whoever he is, he's not worthy of you."

"And you are?" The question left Brian's lips, surprising even him. The man's blue eyes flashed with promise.

"Oh yeah. You should hang out until my shift ends. Let me prove it." Brian eyed his dark hair and deep dimples. Of all the shit he didn't need, this guy topped the list.

*

For several minutes after Brian abruptly ended their call, Terry stared at the green, flashing light on the monitor beside him. He would've thought his heart breaking would at least show a tiny blip on the screen. Even without looking and with the room cast in shadow, he knew Kurt was watching him. He hated knowing the man felt as if he couldn't leave him alone. Looking away from the machine, he focused on Kurt. The glow drifting from the open bathroom doorway glimmered off his eyes, proving he was indeed watching him. It had to be uncomfortable sitting around in a mask all day, hoping not to bring new germs into isolation. Terry could barely hold his lids open against the massive amount of pain medicine pumping through his veins. Drifting into a haze, he heard himself confessing his darkest secret.

"Dying is so much harder than I thought it would be."

"It's not easy from where I'm sitting either." Kurt's words floated through his mind as if part of a dream. When he opened his eyes once more, McKenna was at his side again. Damn. Time slipped away from him here. It could have been a couple of hours or a full day for all he knew. The moment she realized he was awake, she did what McKenna did best—spoke her mind.

"You didn't tell him," McKenna said. There wasn't even a hint of accusation in her voice, only the sure knowledge he had not. "What if you die?" Terry snorted at the question. Anyone else in the world would attempt to assure him he'd pull through, not McKenna. She was honest and forthright to a fault. "I'm being serious, Terry."

He couldn't hide his dry tone. "I know you are." The strain in his voice must have shown because McKenna shot to her feet and helped him snag a quick drink of water. Of course, it didn't stop her lecture.

"He'll hate you forever if you die," she promised. "Mostly because you didn't tell him. He'll be left behind wondering why he wasn't good enough for you to confide in."

"Fine. Goddamn it. Hand me the phone before these damn drugs kick in again."

To say McKenna's smile was triumphant would be the biggest understatement ever uttered by man. She dialed the number before handing him the receiver. As much as Terry would've liked to believe she was trying to help, it was more likely she didn't trust him to really call. It rang four times and he almost hung up. A woman answered.

"Brian Johnson's phone." She was whispering. Glancing at the clock, he calculated the time difference. It was two a.m. in Knoxville.

"Is Brian around?"

"He's sleeping."

"Okay." Terry drew out the word unsure if he was relieved or upset.

"Do you want him to give you a call when he wakes up?"

"No. That's okay. I'll try back later." He didn't bother saying goodbye before hanging up. McKenna's eyebrows couldn't have gone any higher as he handed the phone back to her.

"Who the hell was that?" Her question proved she'd been listening to his every word.

Terry shrugged. "Some woman. I don't know. She didn't give her name."

"Oh. Well. That's okay then. As long as it wasn't another guy, you're good."

Terry wasn't as sure as McKenna

seemed to be, but since he might not live to see the end of the day, what could he say? A wave of panic ran through him. He wasn't ready to die. "If I don't make it, will you tell Brian something for me?"

"Of course."

He tried to come up with something powerful to express how much he loved him. There was nothing. "I have too many things I want to say."

A half-smile played on McKenna's lips. "I guess you'd better pull through then."

"Looks that way." Weariness tugged at him. The meds were kicking into high gear.

Unable to keep from doing so, he closed his eyes. "He was the one," he said before losing the chance. He could hear the way his words slurred. It wouldn't be long now. "Even if I don't make it, he was the one for me."

"I know."

It was the last thing Terry heard.

* * * * *

Someone was trying to drill a hole in his head. It was the only explanation Brian could dredge up for the pain slicing through his brain. A shaft of sunlight blazed through the cracks in the blinds, falling across his face, piercing his skull. As much as he wanted to burrow beneath the blankets, shutting it out, the sound of running water kept him from it. Using a burst of Herculean strength, he pried one eye open. He regretted it immediately. Steam rolled from the open bathroom doorway. Who the hell was in his shower? Fuck. Fuck. Fuck. He couldn't remember anything. What had he done? He ran through a mental check of his body. Other than the pitchfork in his brain, everything else seemed okay. Casting a glance around the room, he checked for any clues to the water-stealing intruder's identity. The only clothes on the floor were his. Wait. He checked beneath the covers and groaned. Goddamn it. Why were his clothes on the floor? A pain hit him in the center in the chest. He was such an idiot. Only a complete moron would ever cheat on Terry. In his panic, he didn't notice the woman's presence until she spoke.

"Good morning."

His heart jumped into his throat. Damn. He really hated it when people snuck up on him. "Good morning," he responded automatically. Something wasn't right. Unless there was some random dude still hiding the bathroom, things were definitely off.

She smiled. "You don't remember me, do you?"

"Uh." The towel wrapped around her head, hid her hair from him, making it impossible to tell the color. Not to mention, the hotel bathrobe hid the rest of her body from head to toe. With his head pounding like it was, there was nothing about her that struck a chord. He honestly had no idea who she was.

Her smile hitched up a notch. "You were pretty messed up by the time we left Julien's Bar and Grill. It took me forever to get you into bed." His mouth fell open at her statement. With a laugh, she pointed at the second full-size bed. "Don't worry. I slept over there." A wave of relief crashed over him. Thank God. He couldn't live with hurting Terry in any way.

Another sharp pain shot through his head. "How much did I have to drink?"

"Not much as I recall."

"Sounds about right."

Her tinkling laughter filled the room. "I'm Kip, by the way."

"Nice to meet you, Kip," he said, allowing his lids to fall closed again. Now that he knew he wasn't in danger of fucking up his life, he could relax. If she was some psycho bent on killing him, she could've done it while he'd been out.

"Terry called while you were asleep."

She knew about Terry. He must have been one hell of a good time. The sound of the man's name had him scrambling for his cell phone. When she gasped, turning toward the wall, Brian almost slapped himself. Right. No clothes. Snagging the sheet, he wrapped it around his hips before snatching up his phone. He scrolled through the call log. There was only one recent call. He didn't recognize the number, but the area code was right.

"Did he leave a message?" She was

eyeing a badly drawn, framed sketch hanging on the wall. "I'm decent. Sort of," he tacked on for good measure, glancing down at the sheet covering his lower half.

She turned around. "He said he'd call back later. I guess I should add he didn't actually say it was Terry but I didn't figure you'd have anyone else calling you at two in the morning."

Brian didn't hesitate or calculate the time difference. No other men called him, period. "It was midnight there but I get what you're saying. He was probably getting back from something."

She gestured toward the phone. "Sorry for answering your cell. I hope I didn't cause a problem, but I hated for it to wake you up since you seemed so out of it last night. You started yelling about being hot and stripping out of your clothes before I could stop you."

Brian tossed the device on the bed before swiping his hand over his eyes, horrified. "Don't worry about the phone. Even if I swung that way, Terry's too conceited to ever suspect me of cheating."

"That's funny."

Not only did she not laugh, he hadn't said anything humorous. Her remark left him confused. "What is?"

She unwound the towel from her hair as she answered. "The way you say he's conceited. It came out sounding like an endearment rather than something most people find repulsive." A mass of wet, red curls fell down her back. Oh. Now he remembered. She was dating the fighter with the blue Mohawk. For the life of him, Brian couldn't remember the guy's name. Of course, the memory of the way he'd left her at the bar without as much as backward glance after an extremely public and loud argument, came rushing back to him. One of these days, he would never drink again. It wasn't for him. He'd been unable to resist helping out a woman in distress. Apparently, he did his best consoling while roaring drunk.

Now that the initial panic passed, the exhaustion came back full-force. He crawled back into bed, curling around the phone as if he could hang onto a wisp of Terry's presence. He closed his eyes, comforted by the thought.

"I love that he's conceited," Brian admitted, hearing the tired note in his own voice. He tugged the blanket over his head to block out the sun, before adding, "Love everything about him."

Chapter Eight

Kip's message was the last he heard of Terry. For three days, Brian made every attempt to get ahold of him without any luck. He'd kept Kip with him for reasons even he didn't understand but he imagined it was something Terry would've done. She was alone and pregnant. Terry would've helped her out. They'd only been in Austin for two days but he had four more days to kill before his next match and they'd be off to the next town. It was a damn good thing he'd won most of his matches. He had some money left in savings, but it wasn't much. The prize money and bonuses he received were the biggest things keeping his ass afloat. Kip was paying her own way and he wasn't sure why she chose to stay. Maybe he needed her more than she needed him. It was a good possibility.

Sequestered in their hotel room, he'd sat at the tiny table beside the window for so long his back had passed beyond cramping an hour earlier. His phone buzzed, moving across the top of the table. He snatched it up, praying he'd see Terry's name. His heart plummeted when Kurt's name appeared instead. Shame filled him over the reaction as he read the text.

"Baby Tayrn is here and healthy. Seven pounds, three ounces and nineteen inches." Brian's response was immediate. "That's awesome. Pics?" He hated that he was having to dredge up a bit of happiness over something he should be ecstatic about. It didn't take long for a series of images to appear across the screen. Everyone he cared about felt so far away.

"She's beautiful."

With his compliments sent, Brian stared at his phone until his pride broke. He sent a message to Terry. "I love you."

The backlighting on his phone slowly faded, going black. Brian still didn't look away. Every second without a response, seemed closer to an hour. He made excuses for him. Most likely he was with McKenna right now. He'd probably turned his ringer off to keep from disturbing such a wonderful family moment. In his heart, Brian knew the truth. They were over.

"I recognize that look," Kip said, interrupting his thoughts. He ignored her. She wasn't deterred in the least. "I know it well," she added. "It's the 'please text me back' stance." Claiming the chair across from his, she mimicked his pose. Leaning forward and resting her forearms on the table, she set her chin on top of her arms.

She stared at the device between them.

"What are you doing?"

"Lending you my will," she answered as if it should be obvious. "Maybe between the two of us we can convince your phone to ring."

Brian scowled. "I know I'm pathetic. There's no need to point it out."

Shifting positions, Kip dug her phone out her back pocket. Placing it face-up next to his, she resumed her watchful stance. "There," she said, sounding satisfied. "If you're a sad case then so am I. At least now neither of us is alone."

He rolled his eyes, but thirty seconds later, her phone lit up when she received an incoming message. In spite of the situation, he chuckled. "I guess you were right. Our combined forces worked for one of us, anyhow."

She slid the device closer, swiping

her finger across the face. For a moment, she simply stared down at it in silence. After a full minute passed, she tucked it beneath her crossed arms before resting her cheek on them. "Yep. I guess it worked."

She kept her gaze focused and unblinking at the opposite wall. He didn't know what to say in the face of her open devastation. He had no idea what that text said, but it had not been good news. It seemed his problems weren't nearly as bad as hers. He hadn't asked about what was going on with the guy who'd abandoned her in Tennessee, and she'd only disclosed enough for him to know the dude had wanted to fuck someone else so Kip was out.

Kip blinked and a tear spilled from the corner of her eye, rolling over her arms before landing on the table. As if the sensation pulled her from her haze she sat up, swiping at her face.

"I guess I'd better start thinking about finding a job and figure out where I'm going from here. It's not like I can keep tagging along with you forever." A strained smile touched her lips.

Brian didn't as much as hesitate. "You'll stay with me until you figure something out."

She shook her head. "I can't expect you to keep this up. You have a life of your own."

"I know that you don't expect anything and I wasn't asking. You'll stick with me."

She leaned back in her chair. "Why?"

"Do you have another option?" He could almost see her searching her mind. When she shook her head, he added,

"Then it's settled." He pushed his phone toward her.

"Terry has a new niece," he said, changing the subject before she could argue. As she scrolled through the pictures, a smile touched her lips even as more tears swam in her eyes.

* * * * *

The guy had a "tell". Every time he threw a punch, his shoulders bunched for a half a second before he led with his right hand. It was all Brian needed to avoid each shot. This shit was almost boring. The other guy was good enough that Brian couldn't seem to pin him but too slow to land a blow. They weren't doing anything more than dancing around on the mat, occasionally getting close enough for bit of dirty boxing. Deciding to play it his way, Brian waited until he'd worn the man down before going low, driving his shoulder into his gut. The double leg takedown was effortless once the guy lost his balance. From there, Brian had him pinned. Easy pickings. There should've been at least an ounce of satisfaction over the win. He searched his heart. There was nothing. Brian focused on the crowd. With the exception of Kip, he didn't know anyone. The sure knowledge he'd be in a different hotel room in a different town by this time tomorrow, settled the matter to his mind. With his decision made, he couldn't wait to get out there. He was going home and Terry would damn well talk to him.

Brian didn't have any trouble exchanging his and Kip's plane tickets to Delaware over to Las Vegas. Kip had been overjoyed at the prospect of settling in one place and agreed it was time for him to confront Terry if he ever hoped to find any peace. The only thing left for him to do was drop the news. He just hadn't decided how to go about it yet. Halfway through packing, his cell phone rang saving him the trouble.

He checked the name before answering. "Hey McKenna. I was just about to call you." The new baby Tayrn was crying in the background. "Uh-oh. Somebody isn't happy," he added, wondering if she could even hear him.

"She doesn't sleep. It makes everyone sad." McKenna's tone was so matter-of-fact Brian chuckled. It wasn't nice of him to laugh at his friend but better her than him. He also found it humorous two such serious people had created a dramatic baby.

"Maybe I can help you out when I get back home since I'll be there by nine a.m." He couldn't hide the excitement in his voice. His words were met with silence.

Even Tayrn stopped fussing. Brian held the phone out, checking to see if the call had been disconnected. The little timer was still running. He pressed it back to his ear.

"Are you still there?"

"Yeah," McKenna answered, sounding hesitant. "It's almost funny. I was calling to tell you I think you should come home."

She had his attention. "Why?"

"I have something I need to tell you."

The way she said it, Brian knew he wouldn't like whatever it was. Even though he didn't need any more bad shit to happen, he still heard himself agreeing. "Okay."

"The thing is, I'm not supposed to tell you. If I do, I'm breaking a promise, but it's something I think you should know, you know?"

"No," he answered, confused.

Her huff rang clear through the line. "You'll be pissed off. I should've called way before now but I didn't know what to do. On one hand, I promised and I do see his point. On the other, sometimes we don't know what best for ourselves. In this case, I don't think he knows what's best."

A sense of foreboding overcame him. They only knew one person mutually who would ask her to keep a secret from him. "Okay," he repeated, incapable of articulating anything further. McKenna groaned.

"Oh. I know," she cried. "How about this? What if I tell you as much as you'll know the moment you set eyes on him? That way you'll be forewarned but I haven't actually given you any details. Therefore, I haven't truly broken my promise. Of course, I really should break it since he told me he would tell you himself but he hasn't and that's wrong."

Brian couldn't stand another moment of the torment. "Is he seeing someone else?"

McKenna didn't hesitate. "No. It's nothing like that. Terry loves you." A wave of relief washed over him. It lasted only long enough for her to take a breath. "He's sick."

Brian's brain failed him in his moment of need. McKenna's words didn't make as much sense as they should have. "He hasn't called me because he's sick?" For some reason, when Brian said it aloud, the impact of the statement hit him. "Wait. How sick are we talking here? I mean, even if I was on my deathbed, I'd like to think I'd find a way to get in touch with him." His question met with nothing but silence. His grip tightened on the phone. "McKenna, how sick is he?"

"I'm glad you're coming home," she answered quietly.

* * * * *

The trip from Texas to Vegas was the longest of his life. No matter how hard he tried, he couldn't get an earlier flight home. By the time they landed at McCarran International and people began pulling down their carry-ons, Brian was ready to barrel his way through them. More than one slow-moving passenger suffered his dark scowl. It didn't help matters that his cell phone wouldn't fucking work on the plane. He might've smashed the damn thing by now if he didn't know how badly he'd need it later.

Kip remained silently at his side. She hadn't tried to comfort him and he appreciated it more than he could say. He was one kind gesture away from a total meltdown. He'd ranted his way through three airports, since for some dumbass reason, they had to change planes in Orlando. Kip simply murmured her agreement when he pointed it out for the hundredth time how ridiculous it was to claim it was more cost efficient to fly hundreds of miles in the opposite direction. The moment his feet hit the terminal, he checked his cell signal again. Seeing he had one bar, he immediately called McKenna.

"I'm here," he said without preamble as soon as she answered. "How is he?"

"Exhausted but the hospital plans to release him today."

His grip tightened on the phone. "Does that mean he's better?"

McKenna ignored his question, making him grind his teeth. "Of course, you know how doctors are. It will probably be later this afternoon before they actually sign off on the paperwork."

He pried his jaw open. No matter how hard he tried, he couldn't bite back the words. "You know, I might not ever be able to forgive you for this." Silence stretched across the line. Brian almost snapped from the tension. Kip touched his arm, drawing his attention and he really looked at her for the first time since rushing her from the hotel. At some point, she'd piled her red curls on top of her head, securing them with a scrunchie, and there were dark smudges beneath her eyes. In spite of his panic, he experienced a pang of regret for the stress he was adding to her life. It wasn't good for the baby.

"Is Terry okay?"

She was more concerned about him than herself he realized with a rush of affection. He didn't deserve her friendship. Shaking his head, he shrugged. She frowned.

"Who is that?" McKenna asked, cutting into the silence. "It's my friend, Kip."

"Bring her to me. You and Terry should have some time alone."

Brian switched his attention back to Kip. "Are you cool with staying with McKenna while I figure things out with Terry?"

"You can drop me at the nearest hotel. I'll be fine. Worry about yourself right now. I've been making my own way for a long time. I just didn't want you to make the trip alone."

Brian rolled his eyes. "She'll be there in half an hour." Kip sighed at his words but didn't argue and Brian didn't back down. "She's in dire need of some

TLC. I've been dragging her all over the country and she's five months pregnant."

"Sounds like we both have some explaining to do," McKenna said in a dry tone.

"No," Brian answered immediately. "Only you." Without waiting for a response, he disconnected the call. After slipping his phone back into his pocket, he relieved Kip of her bag. "Come on. Let's find a cab."

* * * * *

Brian had stopped trying to call and sending him messages three days ago. Even though Terry knew it was for the best, his heart didn't give a shit. The future was nothing but bright lights for Brian. Those days were over for Terry. It did sting a bit to know he'd never get to fight again, but some things were more important—like living.

The moment Terry stepped through the door and he noticed the alarm had been disengaged, he knew. Dread rose in his throat and he tugged his stocking cap down tight. Leaving his suitcase by the back door, he went in search of Brian. He found him in the living room. With his stocking feet kicked up on the coffee table and his fingers linked behind his head, Brian followed Terry with his eyes as he entered the room. He looked tired and so fucking sexy. It made Terry's heart ache. A pair of soft, worn-looking jeans encased his legs. His maroon shirt strained against his biceps.

"You haven't been retuning my calls."

Avoiding his gaze, Terry sat down on the loveseat. "You've been busy. I didn't want to bother you."

Brian didn't respond until Terry met

his stare. "I'm never too busy for you."

Terry didn't say a word. Between travel, training and matches, Brian probably hadn't had a chance to even breathe, but yes, he did know Brian would've dropped everything for him. That was the problem. Terry tried changing the subject, pretending as if this was a social call rather than his judgment day.

"You've kept an eighty-five percent win ratio so I imagine Rhys will be more than happy to accept your challenge." Brian dipped his chin in acknowledgment. He didn't look happy. "Congratulations," Terry added. "I'm proud of you. Not that I haven't always been proud of you," he added, developing a never-heard-before ramble. "Of course, hopefully, you knew that already."

Thankfully, Brian interrupted him before he managed to make a total idiot

215

out of himself. "I have regrets."

The statement made Terry want to plant his fist in the center of Brian's face. There wasn't a single thing he could think of that could've cut more to the bone. He couldn't hold the bitterness on the inside. "I can't believe you regret being with me. Maybe I'm not perfect, but damn. I did think I meant a little something to you." He shook his head, still in disbelief. Fuck. He could've gone his whole life without hearing Brian confess to such a thing. A humorless laugh escaped him. "I'm exhausted." Really. What else could he say?

Brian eyed him a full minute before speaking. "Are you done?"

Terry gestured helplessly, holding his tongue. No. He wasn't finished, but he'd be damned if he begged the man to say it wasn't true.

"I should've asked you to go with me." Terry opened his mouth, ready to say he wouldn't have gone. Brian held up his hand, stopping him. "Then I should have forced you when you refused."

Terry snapped his teeth together, deciding it was useless to point out Brian couldn't force him to do anything he didn't want to do. Brian's lips lifted into a knowing smile as he added, "When you still refused to go, I should've blackmailed you by threatening to never compete again if you didn't come with me." His expression sobered. His eyes seemed almost sad as he admitted, "I hate I didn't do that, because I think I broke something between us by going away."

Terry crossed his arms over his chest as if he could physically protect his heart. He quickly dropped them when he realized the move showed his weakness.

"It's not as if I didn't know I was training you to leave me," he reminded Brian. "I knew." It was silently killing him. Sitting across from Brian while unable to touch him was choking the life from him. "So, you know," he said, incapable of withstanding another second of it. "You're absolved of all guilt or whatever this is. It was nice seeing you again. Have a nice life. Good luck with the title and all that." Terry knew he was taking it too far. Knowing it didn't force him to stop. Brian silently watched him wearing a guarded expression. Damn it. He spent a moment debating if he could actually bite off his own tongue before deciding he liked the taste of food too much. Anything was better than concentrating on the man sitting across from him.

"Are you done?" Brian asked again. With a sharp nod, Terry locked his back teeth together determined he wouldn't say another fucking word. He'd already managed to look like a big enough idiot for the day.

"I went by No Rival today and let Rhys know I wouldn't be challenging him for the title."

"What?"

"As McKenna is overly fond of saying, I believe we speak the same language." Terry's eyes fell closed as a wave of exhaustion washed over him. "You shouldn't have done that." He forced the hoarse words past his rapidly swelling throat. Before he could wuss out, Terry plucked his sunglasses off his head and set them on the table with shaking hands before pulling off his stocking cap. He didn't meet Brian's gaze. "I'm glad you didn't attempt to blackmail me, because I couldn't have gone with you." Shoring up his courage, he met Brian's stare. There wasn't a hint of surprise on his face. He should've known McKenna would eventually say something. Unable to stand it, Terry crossed his arms over his chest, hoping to hold himself together. No one would ever understand how badly he never wanted to do this to Brian. Damn. It really did hurt every bit as much as he feared.

"Why didn't you tell me?"

At Brian's question, Terry wanted to punch a hole in the wall. Why was the man so damn blind? He wanted to give Brian the world. "Because I've got this and you have a championship to win."

In an explosion of fury, Brian shot from his seat. Terry found himself nose to nose with an extremely pissed-off male. Bracing his palms against the couch on either side of Terry's head, he leaned in until he was only inches from his face. Brian spoke through clenched teeth.

"Let's get something straight. Whatever happens to you happens to me, so I ask again, why didn't you tell me?" His nostrils flared. The muscles in his jaw flexed. It was too much for Terry. Having Brian within reach while his heart ached was more than one person could endure. Curling his fingers around the material of Brian's t-shirt, Terry hauled him forward, closing the final gap between them. As his tongue brushed Brian's, he hated himself in that moment. Brian was the one thing he couldn't give up.

Tearing his mouth away, Brian dropped his forehead on Terry's shoulder. Keeping his eyes squeezed shut, Terry absorbed the warmth of his touch. He couldn't look. If he did, Brian might disappear.

"You knew." Even though it came out in a whisper, the accusation in Brian's words couldn't be missed. "You knew before I left but you still let me leave without saying a word." Releasing Brian's shirt, Terry let his hands drop to his lap. It's not as if he could deny it. Brian growled. It was a low and deadly sound. Terry could feel it vibrating from his body. "Goddamn you," he said as he reclaimed Terry's mouth. Against his lips, he repeated, "Goddamn you."

He already had.

*

Rage rolled down Brian's back and churned in his stomach. It filled his mind with a red haze and caused his ears to ring. How could Terry do such a thing? How dare he shut him out? He held onto his anger even as Terry's taste filled his mouth. No amount of fury could douse his love. Terry moaned. The memory of the moment he learned Terry was in the hospital slammed into him. It stole the oxygen from the room. Even though he knew McKenna would never do such a thing, he'd hoped she wasn't telling the truth. He couldn't tell himself that lie any longer. Pulling away, he buried his face against the side of Terry's neck, inhaling his scent. The sound of the other man's breathing was ragged against his ear.

"Tell me," Brian begged, needing to know. He couldn't lose Terry. The world wasn't big enough to contain his grief.

"Non-Hodgkin's. Just like Gray. Apparently, it's not uncommon for it to cluster in families."

His grip tightened on the back of the couch. "Can we fight this?"

"Yes."

Brian slowly released the breath he

hadn't known he was holding. "Then we will."

"Please don't give up your shot at the title because of me."

At Terry's plea, Brian leaned away bringing his face into focus. The light-green eyes that had haunted his dreams begged him to reconsider. "I don't want it," Brian admitted. "I thought I did until it was within reach. The moment I was able to see me taking Rhys' spot, I realized something monumental."

"What's that?"

"I was happier when I was drowning in debt and near to living in a cardboard box because I had you. Without you, it's meaningless and I'm miserable."

"You'll resent me."

"Only if you reject me," Brian shot back without missing a beat. "Either way, I'm out. Maybe I'll take the occasional bout. Perhaps I'll even change my mind one of these days but right now, I don't want it, and I'm absolutely done with leaving you behind. I can live without a lot of things but it turns out you're not one of them."

"I wanted it for you, probably more than you did. That's why I fought as hard as I did to get you ready to go before I was no longer able to do so."

Terry's admission said more than perhaps he meant to reveal. "You've known about this a lot longer than I want to hear, haven't you?"

He winced. "Yeah."

Brian was speechless. He wanted to accuse Terry of making him fall in love under false pretenses. The words wouldn't come. He'd kept his distance. Even their first night together, Terry had tried to walk away before Brian pushed things.

"I didn't want to love you." Terry's whispered confession was the final straw.

"Well I want to love you!" Terry flinched as Brian slammed his hand down on the leather, punctuating his words. He checked his tone, calling his rage under control. "Even if you only have one more day left this on this earth, that one day belongs to me." He couldn't remember a time he'd ever been so furious with anyone.

At his show of temper, Terry's eyes flashed fire. "Do you think I've enjoyed going through this alone?" Brian opened his mouth to answer, but Terry cut him off before he got the chance. "Do you honestly believe I wanted to do weeks of chemo and radiation by myself, living in fear of every phone call, scared of what I'd say? When I said goodbye to you, I knew it might be the last time I'd ever see you again. Do you have any clue how hard that was?" Brian's shirt tightened across his back as Terry balled the material in his hands, pulling him closer until they were nose to nose. "I did it all for you, because you deserve the world. I did it because you are worth more than me."

Terry flattened his palms against Brian's chest and pushed. In his shock, Brian allowed it to happen. He'd been this bad for weeks and no one had said a single thing to him about it. Terry had been sick enough when he left that he thought he might not ever see him again. There were no words to express his fury.

Brian watched in shocked silence as Terry toed off his shoes and unzipped his sweatshirt. He'd lost weight. Brian's mind went numb. Terry was dressed as if it was freezing outside. In truth, for this late in October it was overly warm. The one thing

Brian recalled from his mother's battle with cancer was the way she'd always been cold. Terry peeled his shirt over his head, tossing it on the couch next to the sweatshirt. An angry burn mark marred one side his neck making Brian wince in sympathy.

"Sorry," Terry muttered. "I can't take my collar rubbing at it any longer." He didn't look at Brian nor did he wait for him to respond in any way before walking away. Brian stood in the center of the living room feeling lost. When Terry veered left, into the bedroom, Brian shook off his shock. He trailed after him, stepping through the doorway as Terry climbed onto the bed and fell facedown across it. Speaking into the pillow, Terry grumbled. "I'm tired. You should go tell Rhys you take it back."

"Shut the fuck up, Terry," Brian

snapped as he climbed in beside him, gathering the man against his chest. It was obvious he was having a hard time keeping his eyes open. Brian felt like shit for making him burn so much energy being angry with him. None of it mattered now. They were together.

Chapter Nine

The warm weight against Terry's back seeped into his mind. Still lingering on the edge of sleep, he snuggled closer to it. Brian's arm tightened around his waist, reminding Terry of everything that happened. Instead of fighting it, he soaked up Brian's presence. Every rise and fall of the man's chest pulsed against his back. With their legs entangled, their bodies touched from head to toe. Terry's heart swelled. He'd thought he didn't need anyone. Most certainly, he'd intended on facing this alone. It was almost as if he was testing his bravery. Now that Brian was here, he'd never been more thankful for anything in his life. Missing Brian had been killing him. He was worn out by life, exhausted with the whole goddamn thing.

Covering Brian's arm with his, he

tugged the man as close as he could.

"I didn't come back alone." Terry held still, waiting for Brian to finish his confession. Brian chuckled. The vibration of the sound surrounded Terry. "You're not even going to ask are you?"

Terry smiled into the darkness. He knew Brian too well to believe he'd brought home anyone who threatened their relationship. "Hmm, let me guess. You adopted a stray, didn't you?" Absently, he toyed with Brian's fingers, doing his best not to laugh as the man huffed.

"You really don't think it's even remotely possible you've been replaced, do you?"

"Have I?"

The arm at Terry's waist tightened for a moment at his question.

"Never," Brian answered, sounding

almost vicious, as if the thought pissed him off. Terry brought Brian's hand to his mouth. Pressing his lips to it, he spoke against his skin.

"You brought someone back with you," he reminded him. Terry felt him nod.

"Her name is Kip."

Terry snorted. "You really did adopt a stray."

"Actually, I think her parents might have been hippies." At Brian's confession, Terry rolled onto his back. With his head in his hand, Brian leaned up on his elbow looking down at him. Moonlight streamed through the open blinds, adding just enough light to the room for Terry to see Brian's expression. "So I have your attention now, huh?"

"You always have my attention," Terry admitted.

Brian's eyes hooded at the words.

His expression took on the wicked edge Terry had never been able to resist. He didn't act on it. "She was traveling with Josh something-or-other. I don't know. I always call him Blue Hawk. He's that guy out of Newark. Anyhow, he dumped her off in Tennessee when he found some other woman. I didn't have the heart to leave her there, so I kept her."

As he spoke, Brian traced the line of Terry's abs with his fingertips. Terry didn't think Brian was fully aware of the motion, but he couldn't concentrate on anything else. He forced himself to stay on topic. It was such an ordinary moment for them. He craved it. Nothing had felt normal in a long time.

"It's Josh Salko," Terry supplied, realizing he knew exactly whom Brian was referring. "I know that guy. He's an ass."

Brian watched him in silence for a

moment. "You were in the hospital," he said after a minute, catching Terry off guard with his change in topic and knowledge of the situation.

"I had a massive dose of chemo. It wiped out my healthy blood cells and I overdid it one day. No big deal. Will I trip over this girl on my way to the bathroom?"

"I can't imagine why you would. When did you intend to tell me all of this?"

He didn't see any reason to lie. "I didn't have a plan. You said you didn't come back alone and this is your home. It stands to reason you've stashed her in one of the spare bedrooms. From there, I assumed I would be tripping over her soon."

Brian blinked several times as if rendered speechless. The unconscious touch at Terry's waist was still driving him insane. He covered Brian's hand with his, stopping the motion. The contact seemed to loosen Brian's tongue.

"Since when is this my home?"

"I gave you a key," Terry reminded him. "We moved your things in."

Brian stared past him toward the wall, seeming lost in thought. "When you didn't answer any of my texts, I thought you were finished with me."

Irritated, Terry slipped from his hold and out of the bed. He went straight for the closet. After opening the door, he flipped on the light and gestured toward Brian's clothes. "Your side of the closet." From there, he moved to the dresser, opening a few of the drawers. "All yours," he pointed out. Moving to the bathroom, Terry switched on the light as he entered the room. He made a show of going through the cabinet's contents. "Yep. You have stuff in here as well." Brian came to stand in the doorway. He leaned against the doorframe, watching Terry make his point.

"One minute you tell me you thought you might not ever see me again when I left, and the next you say this is my home. I don't know how you expect me to not be confused." Although Brian's tone remained level, Terry knew Brian too well. He was barely restraining his temper.

Grasping the edge of the counter, Terry bowed his head. He stared at his whitening knuckles, unsure of the right thing to do. Brian would either get pissed or he wouldn't, Terry decided. He drew a deep breath for strength before meeting Brian's gaze.

"If I don't make it, McKenna gets everything," he paused before adding, "except this house. It's yours. Asher has all the paperwork."

*

Brian had nothing. He could tell by the set of Terry's jaw he was braced for the worst. Brian couldn't think of a single thing to say in response. "I don't understand." He heard himself. It was a dumbass thing to say. He knew it, but he was floored. Before Terry could call him on it, he added, "I mean I do, but..." He gestured helplessly. "I don't."

Terry pushed away from the counter, moving to stand in front of him. "I love you."

Brian didn't hesitate. "I love you too." It was the only thing through everything that he never questioned.

"Then do this for me."

He didn't know what to say. In the face of Terry's plea, he was helpless. All of the emotion he'd been trying to suppress rushed to the surface, choking him. "You can't leave me."

Terry reached for him and massaged the side of his neck as if attempting to soften the blow of his words. "You can't make me stay. I wish it was that easy, but it's not. All I'm asking is for you not to fight me on this. Let me have this tiny ounce of comfort, knowing our home will still be ours even if I'm no longer in it."

He didn't have a choice. How could he say no? "You don't play fair."

At his accusation, Terry smiled. "I warned you. Lesson number one—I always get what I want."

"Then you should want to live," Brian shot back.

The smirk Brian had always found irresistible made an appearance. "I do."

Some of the tightness eased in Brian's chest. Terry was right. He did always get his way. Terry's thumb brushed along the column of Brian's neck reminding him of how close he stood.

"Are you still tired?"

Terry shook his head.

"Good," Brian said as he eyed the man's mouth. "I need a shower. I haven't had one since before I checked out of the hotel." He searched his mind in an attempt at recalling the time. He gave up. "Whenever that was."

A flash of disappointment crossed Terry's face but he didn't argue. He made a move as if to leave. Brian braced his arm against the doorframe, blocking his path. "Where do you think you're going?" He dropped his hand from the frame to Terry's waist, tugging him closer. "I'm not letting you out of my sight. You have a habit of disappearing."

One corner of Terry's mouth lifted in a sardonic smile. "If that's the only reason you want me to stay..."

Brian worked the button free on Terry's jeans. "Do you really want me to give you a list of reasons? It could take a while." He slid the zipper down. "I could show you instead." Dipping his head, he captured Terry's mouth with his. Every frayed nerve and hurt Brian suffered in the past weeks smoothed away as Terry sank his teeth into his bottom lip. His fingers closed around Terry's erection.

"Shower later."

Brian chuckled at the demand while doing his best to drive Terry insane. The material of his shirt slid up his back as Terry hands dove beneath it. He backed away long enough to pull it over his head before recapturing Terry's mouth. The man's jeans had to go, Brian decided, pushing them down his hips. Brian felt him flinch. Scared he'd done something wrong, Brian tore his mouth away, glancing down. A huge bruise covered Terry upper thigh.

"It's the only place they can give me some of my injections," Terry said. His tone and expression made Brian's chest hurt. It was as if he thought he was ruining their moment by explaining the mark.

"Anything else I need to know about?" As Brian asked the question, his hands went to his own jeans, working on the button. Terry's eyes followed the motion.

"Not that I can think of."

"Good. Finish getting undressed."

Without waiting to make sure he complied, Brian kicked out of his clothes and headed for the shower. With the door standing open, he twisted the knobs until a hint of steam rolled from the water falling from the showerhead. A solid weight landed between his shoulder blades, shoving him inside. Terry followed him in, pulling the door closed behind them. Brian turned in enough time to catch sight of Terry's determined expression before his back hit the shower wall. Snagging his neck, Terry consumed him. There was no other way to describe the devouring kiss.

His fingers dug into Brian's nape as Terry held him in place, controlling the pace. He palmed Brian's cock with the other, leaving him incapable of doing anything other than holding on for the ride. He gripped Terry's hips. His body became a mass of nerve endings sending him into sensory overload. Out of control didn't come close to describing what it was like to be with Terry. Brian could jack off a million times and never recreate the sensation of Terry's fingers wrapped around his dick. Every time he ventured near the edge of orgasm, Terry slowed his pace, drawing him back. It was the sweetest torture. In an attempt at getting even, Brian towed him closer. With a roll of his hips, he allowed the friction of their wet skin to brush Terry's dick, drawing a satisfying moan from his throat. He should've known it wouldn't be that easy. Terry released his hold. With the wall holding him up, Brian watched through half-closed lids as Terry squirted a generous amount of body wash in his hand. He swiped it over Brian's skin until it foamed, slipping down his frame. The expression Terry wore was hot as hell as he followed the motion of his hands with his eyes. It was obvious he was every bit as ready to explode as Brian, but he didn't rush.

Brian experienced an odd mixture of impatience and steady calm. He wanted everything, and he needed it now, but he equally savored every second. Terry seemed so absorbed in his task, when he spoke it startled Brian.

"You're like a sickness for me." His gaze lifted from where he watched his hands to Brian's face. The earnestness of his words shined in his eyes. "I'm addicted to being in love with you."

It was as if Terry managed to describe every one of Brian's emotions in a single sentence. There wasn't a cure or rehab he could enter. Terry was a permanent affliction. Brian nodded. "For real, you're under my skin."

He couldn't stand another second without tasting Terry. He closed the distance between them, taking Terry's bottom lip between his. Sliding his tongue across it, Brian savored the texture. He repeated the motion until he coaxed Terry into chasing after him. The moment he did, Brian sealed his mouth over Terry's, matching him stroke for stroke. He pulled away long enough to rinse away the soap and turn the water off.

"No more teasing," he said as he reclaimed Terry's mouth. Without giving up his prize, he reached past Terry and pushed the shower door open. He urged him backward. Terry moved but it wasn't quick enough to Brian's way of thinking. When he switched from Brian's lips to his jaw, Brian heard himself beg. "Please? I've been missing you for too long." At his confession, Terry ripped open the bathroom drawer and pulled out a handful of condoms. Brian didn't stop moving. He refused to give Terry time to close it. A low laugh slipped past his lips when Brian nearly barreled him down. At the sound, Brian made a second confession. "I need to feel you inside me."

They didn't make it to the bed. Utilizing a flawless ankle pick, Terry hooked Brian's foot with his, taking him down on the bedroom floor. As if a testament to the man's controlled strength, even in his weakened state, Terry ensured Brian landed softly on the carpet. Terry followed him down. Brian flattened his palms against the floor beside him in an attempt to cling to his sanity as Terry kissed a path down his body. With his focus locked on the things Terry was doing to him, Brian swore he could feel every single one of Terry's taste buds swiping over his skin.

Wet heat closed around the crown of his dick. His hips left the floor, fingers digging into the carpet. He barely registered the sound of Terry ripping open the condom. His body was on fire. Drawing his knees up, Brian lost himself in the sensation of Terry's throat tightening around his cock. Terry dipped lower. He lapped at Brian's balls before moving to circle his asshole with the tip of his tongue. Brian fought to drag air into his lungs. A noise came from deep inside him. He was helpless to stop it from leaving his lips. As if it was what Terry had been waiting for, he shifted positions. Between Brian's thighs, Terry held his stare as he pressed his way inside. His heavy-lidded gaze had Brian reaching down and fisting his own cock. The things Terry did to his body were secondary to what he did to Brian's mind.

"Let me have it."

At Terry's demand, Brian's skin pulled tight for half a second before an orgasm crashed over him. Terry's eyes fell closed as hot liquid filled the space between them, coating both their stomachs. Brian couldn't tear his eyes away from the man above him as the tremors ran through him and Terry pumped inside him. A line formed between his brows and the cords in his neck stood out, signaling Terry had reached the edge.

Brian strained against him determined to leave him gasping. When Terry released a hoarse cry, Brian moved up onto his elbows. Capturing Terry's mouth, he did his best to memorize the way the sound felt against his tongue. Hooking Brian's knee with his forearm, Terry rolled, taking Brian with him. He found himself straddling Terry's hips.

After one final brush of lips on lips, Brian set his forehead against Terry's, inhaling his presence into his lungs. In a desperate attempt at expressing the emotion bursting from inside him, Brian said the first that came to mind, "You make me dream."

He didn't know how else to explain the way Terry made him envision endless days of living exactly as they were right now. Terry cupped his face, forcing him to hold his stare. "Sixty years." The force in which Terry said the two words left Brian with no doubt that it had been a vow. "Everyone promises forever," he explained. "I swear I will give you at least sixty years."

Brian couldn't breathe. He recognized the look of determination in Terry's eyes. It was the same one he'd seen when he'd been bent on training him. In that moment, Brian knew if Terry never did another thing, he would give him the sixty years he'd promised simply because he'd vowed to do so.

Swallowing past the lump growing in his throat, Brian nodded. "Sixty years," he agreed.

* * * * *

"Where's Terry?" Kip asked around a bite of toast.

"He's still sleeping." As if needing to make a liar of him, Terry rounded the corner. A smile lit his face at the sight of them sitting at the kitchen island.

"Who's still sleeping?" Terry asked, kissing Brian before he had a chance to answer. Shirtless and wearing a pair of jeans still unbuttoned at the waist, Terry made Brian want to whimper because they weren't alone.

With her toast halfway to her mouth, Kip gave Terry a small wave the moment he came up for air. "Hi."

"You must be Kip."

Brian could hear the laughter in

Terry's voice. Brian comforted himself that he hadn't been lying about her not being stashed in one of the spare bedrooms. He'd called her the moment he'd gotten out of bed, giving her the all-clear and Cameron, who'd been there visiting, had brought her straight over. Cameron hadn't stayed long and since he was in his police uniform, Brian assumed he was on his way to work. If Kip was the least bit uncomfortable with being surrounded by strangers, she didn't utter a word of complaint.

"I am. You must be Terry." He winked in answer, turning his back on them to grab a drink out of the fridge. Kip caught Brian's eye, mouthing "wow" before Terry could catch her. A ridiculous rush of heat hit his face. Dropping the toast, Kip cleared her throat. "Don't worry. I don't intend to take over your home.

McKenna said she'd give me a job at the bookstore and I'll start looking for an apartment right away."

Terry leaned back against the counter. Crossing one ankle over the other, he shook the small bottle of orange juice while silently assessing her. "Is Josh the father of your baby?"

At Terry's question, Kip's expression went blank. Brian knew how much she hated talking about her problems. "What does that have to do with anything?" she asked in a hollow tone, avoiding his question.

"You'll stay here."

Brian wanted to laugh. Kip's expression turned mutinous at Terry's announcement and he knew she was about to see the stubborn side of the man Brian loved.

"I can't invade your home like that.

It's not right."

Terry tilted his head to the side but his expression remained bland. "Says who?"

"Says me," Kip shot back.

"Since it's my home being invaded, your opinion doesn't count."

Kip looked at Brian obviously seeking help. He smiled. Terry drank his juice, unfazed by her ire. "You said he was conceited. You didn't say he was bossy too."

Terry smirked. Damn. Brian had missed that look. "I'm all things magnificent," Terry said, setting the bottle aside before adding, "and Josh is crazy. When he comes to his senses, and he will, he'll be looking for you. Do you really intend to stand against him without any protection?"

Brian could see her beginning to

panic. When her shoulders squared, Brian almost groaned.

"I'm assuming by your statement, you intend to be around that long." Brian sucked in a hiss. At the sound, Kip met his gaze. "I'm not taking it back. Have you asked him? I mean straight up asked him if he's going to die? You deserve to know the truth."

"Kip," Brian began but Terry cut him off.

"No. It's okay. She's right." He moved to stand behind Brian. Wrapping his arms around him, Terry set his chin on Brian's shoulder. Tilting his head, Brian brought Terry's face into focus. He was staring at Kip. Brian held his breath. "I need a stem cell transplant and a drug that hasn't been approved by the FDA yet. Without that, yes, I will die." Brian's eyes fell closed and Terry's hold tightened. "I'm on a waiting list. The drug company is only allowed to release this medicine to a set number of people each year while it's still in the testing stages but I've promised Brian sixty years and I still owe him sixty-one of those so I have faith." Brian couldn't believe how much humor Terry had in his voice as he said the words.

"How does that work?"

Kip sounded genuinely interested. Brian still couldn't open his eyes. Reality looked too bleak. Terry pressed his lips to his cheek several times. He could feel the smile shaping the man's lips in each kiss. The final one landed near his ear and lingered.

"I promised," Terry whispered against his skin and Brian's chest squeezed. He opened his eyes, unable to hold back a smile at the words. Terry wouldn't leave him. Obviously having received the desired effect, Terry switched his attention back to Kip. "It's like this. I said I'd give him sixty years of my life so I have to live at least—"

Kip waved a dismissive hand, cutting off his explanation. "I meant your treatment. Tell me how that works."

"Sure. Seeing as how I don't have any close relatives there's little to no chance of me ever being able to find a matching stem cell donor, so the doctors have to use my own. Basically, they'll remove my piddling amount of stem cells and freeze them. I'll get a massive dose of chemo and radiation to kill the cancer. Once it's dead, they'll give me back my stem cells along with the new drug. It will help me grow new, fat, healthy and cancer-free cells. All better," he finished with a flourish.

"How long will it take for you to get

approved for this medicine?"

She had all the tough questions and Brian was glad for it since he didn't think he could make his throat work properly at the moment. He felt the change in Terry. Some of the happiness left his voice when he answered.

"It could be a long wait. You know how the government holds shit up."

Brian kept his gaze locked on Kip's face. He wanted to look at Terry but he was scared of what he would see in his expression. Kip chewed on her bottom lip. Staring off into space, she seemed to turn the problem over in her mind. When she met Brian's stare once more, a look of determination entered her eyes before she switched her attention to Terry.

"How concerned are you over the legality of obtaining this drug?"

"I promised Brian sixty years," Terry

repeated as if it explained exactly how far he would go, and indeed, it did.

Kip nodded. Twisting in her seat, she snagged her purse from the back of the barstool. Brian watched in silence as she dug around inside coming out with her cell phone. Terry brushed his fingertips along Brian's arm in an absent motion as he too watched Kip's every move. Brian absorbed the sensation of Terry's touch. Kip's fingers moved over the phone for a minute before she seemed to find what she was looking for. She set the device on speaker and left it sitting on the island. As it rang, she glanced at Terry.

"Write down the details of what you need." Even though neither of them understood what was going on, Terry moved away to do as she said, digging around in the junk drawer until he came up with a pad of paper and pen at the same time Kip's call was answered.

"Hello."

At the sound of the man's heavy Russian accent, an affectionate smile touched Kip's lips. "Konstantin."

"Kipley," the man breathed, sounding entirely too satisfied. "How have you been?" Kip tilted her chin back and blinked rapidly at the ceiling as she answered.

"Oh, you know me. I always land on my feet. I got to ride in a police car this morning."

A loud litany of Russian rang through the line. Kip released a watery laugh as the tears she'd been holding back spilled over her lashes.

"Yes. I know it wasn't a first for me, but I was riding up front this time and it certainly did bring back memories."

The man continued speaking in

Russian even though Kip answered in English. It was obvious she understood his every word. Terry handed her the paper. She nodded her thanks, swiping at her cheeks and continuing to listen to whatever the man was saying. When it became apparent, he didn't intend to slow, Kip interrupted him.

"Konstantin, I need something. It's important." Her words were met with heavy silence. Kip chewed on her bottom lip again.

"Tell me."

At his barked command, Kip's eyes closed in obvious relief and she explained the situation before adding in the details Terry had written down for her. After she spelled the name of the medicine for him, he switched back to speaking Russian and Kip glanced at her watch, nodding.

"Yes. That's good." She paused a

moment before adding, "Thank you. This means the world to me."

"Ah. Kipley. It pleases me to bring you pleasure." There was no mistaking the innuendo. It was as if Kip turned inside herself at the statement. A sardonic smile twisted her lips. When she spoke again, it was barely a whisper.

"But the price is so high."

"Oh my love," he said, sounding sad. "Nothing in this world is free. Eventually we all must pay up, eh?"

"Yes," she agreed.

"You are not allowed to be sad. Now, I must go move the mountains and make you smile again. Goodbye for now."

"For now," Kip agreed as she pushed the phone away, appearing almost unwilling to look at either of them. They were both watching her intently. "The two of you should go back to bed," she said after a minute, still not looking at them.

Terry made an impatient gesture. "Being as how I just got up, I'm not feeling especially tired. However, I am experiencing an overload of curiosity mixed a huge helping of what the hell is going on?"

Brian nodded. "Yeah. What he said."

She toyed with the napkin at the edge of her plate. "I didn't say a word about sleeping. The two of should go back to bed and enjoy your time together. In about twenty-four hours or so, your name will hit the top of that list and you'll have to head back to the hospital for treatment if you don't want to miss your turn."

Kip managed something Brian never thought he'd live to see. Terry's mouth fell open in surprise. She'd robbed him of speech. Brian was scared to hope and something didn't feel right. Kip didn't seem happy for someone who'd just arranged a miracle. Even after she'd been abandoned in a bar by the father of her baby, Brian had never seen her look as broken as she did now.

"Who was that?"

Her lips twisted. "I'm not sure you really want to know the answer to that. Now, seriously, go spend some time with Terry before he has to go."

"He will," Terry answered for him. "After you answer his question, who was that on the phone?"

"Konstantin Danshov."

She was right. They didn't want to know. Konstantin Danshov had—at one time— been one of hockey's greatest players until he was discovered running a sophisticated drug ring inside the US and was deported back to Russia to stand trial. Even with his player status, the news might have died down before someone like Brian ever remembered his name. That is, until it came to light after his deportation that he was a member of the Russian mafia. Not some flunky either, but someone who got things done. From what Brian understood, the man had been good looking and charming. Those two traits had carried him far. Once he was out of the hands of the US government, his position left him free of any punishment for his crimes. Brian didn't know what to say. Obviously mistaking his silence for condemnation, Kip spoke up.

"How much do you remember about the night I helped you back to your room from the bar?"

"Not much," Brian admitted. Terry snorted but Brian refused to look over at him. He could feel his knowing laughter. Kip gave him a luminous smile.

"All the way back to the room, you ran down the list of reasons why you were outraged over the knowledge Terry was slipping away from you. Right before you passed out, a sense of peace seemed to settle over you." She made a helpless gesture. "I don't know how else to explain the complete shift in your mood. Even though you were beyond fucked up, you looked at me seeming completely lucid and said, "I'm not sorry. Even at his worst, he's better than everyone else and for a little while, he was mine."

"I don't remember that," he admitted before adding, "but I don't doubt it. Terry is better than everyone else."

"I love you," Terry said, cutting into their conversation. Brian glanced over, surprised by Terry's fierce tone. Terry was watching him as if he'd been waiting for him to meet his gaze. When he had Brian's attention, he added, "so fucking much. It would kill me if you regretted me."

Brian shook his head. "Never," he swore.

With a smile, Terry switched his attention back to Kip. "So, he's your friend?"

Even though there hadn't been an ounce of judgment in Terry's tone, Kip's expression turned ferocious, as if daring anyone to mock her as she answered. "I'm not sorry. He's a bad person, but he wasn't when it came to me, and he was the one. I've accepted I'll never see him again and I've moved on, but I'll never move on, you know?"

Terry motioned toward the phone. "Where there's a connection, there's hope."

"No." Kip shook her head and then she repeated the word as if making it real.

"No. There isn't, but that's sweet. Now, seriously guys, please go away and let me sulk in private." Brian could tell Terry didn't want to believe, didn't want to hope. Obviously, Kip saw it as well. "Trust me, if you need something taken care of, there is no one better than Konstantin. Friends in low places with friends in high places are the best to have."

Brian was skeptical too but he wouldn't turn down a chance to spend the day with man he loved.

He pushed his stool away from the island and moved to Terry's side. "Come on," he said, urging him away. Terry didn't budge. Instead, he eyed Kip questioningly.

"Will you be okay?"

Kip pulled a strained smile. "Don't worry about me. Seriously," she added when Terry didn't look convinced.

"All right," he said, giving in. "Even

if they don't call, it means more than I can say that you tried, and I wasn't joking, you're staying here." It couldn't have been more obvious Terry believed that call would never come.

Kip gave a jerky nod and Terry finally headed back down the hall. Brian pulled Kip into a bear hug.

"Thank you."

She patted his arm. "I don't want to cry again. Go away." With a chuckle, he moved to do as she bade. Her phone beeped drawing his attention before he could take a step. Out of pure habit, he glanced down. Konstantin's name appeared. If the text had been longer, Brian might have missed it or at least he would've attempted to tear his gaze away without reading it. As things were, the two-word message was impossible to miss.

Meet me.

In his shock, he didn't have time to look away before another text appeared beneath the first.

Action Heliport on Las Vegas Blvd. in two hours.

"I thought he'd been deported." Silence met his statement. Before he could change his mind, Brian retrieved his keys from the hook by the back door. He set them on the table next to her phone. "The gold one is for the back door. The silver is for the front. My car is in the garage. I don't want you stuck here without a way to get around." Without waiting for a response, Brian went in search of Terry.

*

Terry stared at the ceiling doing his best to keep his mind blank. In spite of his best efforts, his heart raced along with his thoughts. He couldn't let himself believe. The disappointment would be too much when it came. The sound of Brian closing the bedroom door drew his attention, giving him something else to focus on. As he crossed the room, Brian tugged his soft, gray t-shirt over his head and tossed it aside. His body was harder than it had been when he'd left. The months of constant training and back-to-back bouts had caused a slight change in him. He intended to give up his chance at the title. The knowledge didn't sit well with Terry, but one battle at a time.

At the foot of the bed, Brian paused. "I have to know. Is this thing meant to be sat on?"

Terry craned his neck as if he could see the bench Brian referred. It was too low. Not that it mattered since he saw the thing every day. "I have no idea," Terry admitted, causing Brian to bark out a laugh. At the sound, Terry added,

"Honestly. I'm a bit scared to find out."

Brian shook his head as he climbed onto the bed. He crawled across until he was straddling Terry's hips. At the last second, he seemed to remember the bruises on Terry's thighs and moved higher. Sitting back on his heels, he pinned Terry to the bed while keeping his weight balanced on his knees. Terry appreciated his efforts. As a matter of point, he was thankful for a lot when it came to Brian. Terry stared up into the face of the man above him, doing his best to memorize every nuance. The sharp angles, full lips and eyes that were an indescribable shade of light brown mixed with amber, combined to make Brian almost as gorgeous on the outside as he was on the inside. That was saying something. There was a tiny scar above his left eyebrow where it had obviously been pierced at some point. He had a hard time picturing it, but he also imagined it had been sexy as hell.

"I missed you. Have I told you that enough times already?"

Although Brian had said it a time or two, he'd never get tired of hearing it. "I missed you too." The admission led to another as Terry suddenly wanted Brian to know his every secret. "I gave up competing because I found out I had cancer." His gaze shifted from Brian's face to the flat pads of his chest. He couldn't look him in the eye and say things he'd never told another soul. "A week before Gray died I was diagnosed with early stage Non-Hodgkin's. It was treatable and as far as diagnoses go, it wasn't that bad. Nonetheless, the radiation and chemo weren't a walk in the park either. I retired. That's how I met Anna and Betty, by the way. Nobody knew. McKenna was avoiding me and I wouldn't have burdened her with it even if she hadn't been. Gray's death was still too fresh." He paused, swallowing against the emotions brought on by the memories of that time in his life. "Anyhow, it seemed as if I was always scheduled for chemo at the same time as Anna. Truly, it's as tedious as hell. Eventually, you sort of feel like you know everyone there. We started talking one day as if we'd always known one another." A bitter smile tugged at the corners of his mouth. "So, yeah, that's why I took her death the way I did. It was just so unfair, you know. She was a teenager and a good person."

Thankfully, Brian stayed quiet, giving him the time he needed to work through his thoughts. It was harder than Terry had been expecting, but Brian deserved to know everything. He was incapable of holding back the rush of anger overwhelming him when he looked at things too closely.

For the first time in his life, Terry wanted what Brian offered with his silent strength—a safe place to express his fury. "Gray was a good person too. It didn't seem to count for anything and that really pisses me off. In my life, I've met so many people who are the lowest pieces of shit and waste of good air. They always breeze through life while the truly amazing people do nothing but suffer one setback after another. Not long before we met, I started having chest pains and days when I didn't want to get out of bed. In the back of my mind, I knew, but I tried to pretend as if it wasn't happening. There was a small part of me that thought to simply let nature run its course. The day Anna died, I knew it was time to face it. When I found out I was right and it was worse than before, at least I knew, unlike Anna and Gray, I'd done plenty of things in my life to deserve it."

"No," Brian said, surprising Terry with the anger in his tone. Getting down in his face, he braced his weight on his palms until Terry didn't have any choice except to look him in the eyes. There was only honesty and love in his gaze. "What I told Kip was the truth. You are better than everyone else is. I didn't say that because I'm in love with you. I fell in love with you because it's true."

It went against everything inside him to show even a hint of weakness but he couldn't hold back. "What if I used up the last of my good luck when I got you?"

A hint of a smile passed over Brian's features. "Nope. It was all preordained. I realized it while Kip was making that phone call. Being in this situation caused you to see something in me the day we met and you didn't stop until you had me ready to head out on my own. When I did, I met Kip. It was all meant to happen exactly the way it has. This thing between us, it wasn't some accidental clashing of souls or whatever." He shook his head, as if he didn't know how to explain it. Terry got it. "It was all part of a bigger plan."

Terry wanted to believe Brian. No way did he intend to fail him but if he did—damn. He couldn't leave him feeling the way Gray had left McKenna, as if it was somehow her fault. "You're perfect. You know that right?" Terry asked in a desperate attempt to make Brian see what he did.

Brian closed the final gap between them, touching his lips to the corner of Terry's mouth and placing light kisses there. "Only in your eyes," he said before moving to the other corner of Terry's mouth. It wasn't true but Terry had time to make him see. He could argue later.

As things were, he was having a hard time concentrating on anything with Brian's lips clinging to his. He didn't attempt to deepen their kiss. It was driving Terry insane.

The harder he tried to tempt Brian, the lighter Brian's touch became. The man possessed an unnatural talent. No one kissed the way he did. It was the stuff of fantasies. No way had anyone ever willingly walked away from him and he belonged to Terry. A rush of possessiveness ran through him. Snagging the back of his neck, Terry held Brian in place as he lifted his head and did his best to deepen their kiss. The bastard chuckled.

Not only did Brian know what he'd been doing, he still managed to find a way to torture Terry by refusing to completely meet him stroke for stroke. With one final nip at his bottom lip, Terry gave up. Splaying his arms wide, he let his head drop back to the pillow, showing his surrender.

"Fine, tease, I'm at your mercy."

As the final word left his lips, Brian slammed his mouth over Terry's, pushing his way inside. Brian's tongue stroked his boldly. The world disappeared. They could've been anywhere for any length of time. Terry wouldn't have known or cared. There was nothing left except the way he felt. He was a bundle of emotion and sensations. Brian moved to Terry's jaw, trailing kisses to his ear.

"I'm not teasing now. Kip said we have one day. For the next twenty-four hours, I'm all about pleasing you. Tell me what you want and I'm your man."

The offer was such a broad one and Terry's heart was in charge. "Anything I want?" Brian's lips closed around his lobe. Each breath he released blew across Terry's ear. His body responded as if it was happening to his dick. It was getting harder to speak, but he needed Brian to clarify his offer. "No matter what it is?"

"Mm," Brian hummed against his throat as he moved further down. Terry took it as a yes.

"I want to marry you." Every single muscle in Brian's body tensed. Terry was fairly certain he'd stopped breathing. He wouldn't take it back. Next to having a long life, this was the one thing he wanted more than anything. Brian slowly lifted his head, meeting his gaze. He looked stunned. "We're only an hour away from the California state line, three hours from San Bernardino. We could be there and back long before the twenty-four-hour mark," Terry added when Brian didn't respond. Brian moved back to sitting on his heels. His gaze never left Terry's face. Underneath the weight of his silence, Terry cracked. "I'm sorry. We've never really talked about it and I had no right to spring it on you like that."

Brian's eyes flared, showing his temper. "Do you love me?"

Terry floundered at the ridiculous question. "You know I do."

"Then you have every right," Brian snapped. "You caught me off guard, but fuck yeah. I want to marry you. You're the other half of me."

Chapter Ten

It was amazing how much a person could accomplish in a few hours given the proper motivation. With Brian's agreement, Terry was highly motivated. In a matter of nine hours, they managed to hop a quick flight, buy rings, exchange vows and fly back home. On the way to California, they'd decided Brian would take Terry's last name. After placing a quick call to Asher, he confirmed their decision. Terry wanted to ensure Brian would be treated with the respect due a husband when he reentered the hospital. It was the only decision he'd made while speaking with his lawyer that Brian agreed with. To be on the safe side, Asher was drawing up papers to make sure Brian would have power of attorney. In a not-so-agreed-upon move, Terry asked Asher to change his will. Brian was pissed with him over it but trying hard not to show it. Terry had tried explaining his reasoning, but Brian was still silently seething. As his husband, if Terry didn't make it, Brian would be left with all his financial obligations. Even if someone was opposed to a same-sex marriage, they had no qualms about sending the spouse a bill. There was no way Terry would let a little way-of-the-world technicality get in the way of his wedding night. A smile stretched his lips at the thought. Brian really was his now.

Since they'd left Brian's car for Kip, they'd taken Terry's truck. With Brian behind the wheel, Terry was free to watch the man's every move.

"You're staring at me," Brian said without looking.

Terry's smile hitched up a notch. As

dark as it was, he didn't know how Brian could tell. "I'm waiting on you to figure out I'm right and stop being angry."

"I'm not mad." It was a blatant lie, but Brian glanced his way as if it would lend truth to the words. Terry let it stand.

"That's too bad. I was looking forward to coaxing you into a better mood." Instead of the laughter Terry had been expecting, Brian snapped.

"Well. Really, Terry, what the fuck?" He punctuated this litany by smacking his palm against the steering wheel. "I feel like everyone will think I want your money."

In a move that could only be described as dumbass, Terry snorted. He tried to cut the sound off, but the attempt only ended up making it sound louder in the otherwise silent truck. A muscle in Brian's jaw flexed. "I'm sorry. I'm not mocking your concerns, but they are ridiculous. You do realize we're married now, right? That means, what's mine is yours and what's yours is mine. What difference does it make if I'm alive or dead?"

Brian didn't respond. Instead, he kept his gaze locked on the road. Terry comforted himself that Brian's jaw wasn't jumping and his nostrils had stopped flaring. Out of pure devilment, Terry refused to stop staring at him. They were close to the house. Brian wouldn't stand this much longer. It would be worth it when the man finally snapped. He kept too much passion bottled inside him and Terry did enjoy being on the receiving end of his storm. It was like he couldn't stop stirring the pot. "To be fair, I inherited a majority of my money. If you're that uncomfortable with it then you'd better get busy snagging that title. With the right sponsorship, you could easily clear a million every time you entered the cage." The tic was back. Brian probably wouldn't have any enamel left on his teeth if he held his tongue much longer. Terry smirked. He couldn't help it. Brian might be irritated, but he wasn't arguing. It was only a matter of time before he came around to Terry's way of thinking.

The door to the garage slid open as they turned into the driveway. Brian's car was gone. "Kip must've gotten bored." Brian held steady in his silence. With a heavy sigh, Terry climbed out the truck. The garage door's motor, as it worked toward closing it behind them, was the only sound inside the building as Terry headed for the side door. He knew Brian was right behind him every step of the way because he could feel the man's angry stare boring into the back of his neck.

As always, the exhaustion hit unexpectedly. The trip had taken a lot more energy than he had to spare but it had been worth it. Even if it killed him, he wouldn't let it ruin their night. Unfortunately, as the garage went quiet, the sound of his heart beating pulsed loudly inside his ears. His steps slowed. By the time he made it inside the house, he was sure he was moving at a crawl. Brian's arms encircled his waist from behind. Terry surrendered more of his weight than he intended against Brian's chest. Brian steered them toward the couch.

"Do you know one of things I missed the most while I was gone?" Brian asked.

Terry was thankful Brian didn't wait for an answer. He was having a hard time catching his breath.

"This couch," Brian finished.

Shifting positions, he dropped down into his usual spot, pulling Terry along with him and tucking him against his side. Releasing the footstool, he continued as if nothing out of ordinary was happening. "I mean it's ridiculous to miss a piece of furniture, but this one is special, you know." He toed off his shoes and Terry did the same, allowing them to simply fall off the side onto the floor. With his weight on his hip, Terry relaxed against Brian's chest enjoying the sound of his heart beating against his ear.

"I'm sorry," Terry said as soon as he caught his breath.

"You should be," Brian said sounding calm and taking Terry by surprise. "It was a total dick move using the title shit against me."

"That's not what I meant."

"Sure it is," Brian shot back, before

adding, "Seeing as how you have nothing else to be sorry about and that's how it works. You act like an ass over my career. It pisses me off. You apologize and everything's better. See?"

In spite of the situation, Terry chuckled. His good humor only lasted long enough for reality to set back in. "I wanted this night to be different."

At his admission, Brian lifted Terry's hand from where it rested on his stomach, bringing it to his lips. Keeping their fingers linked, he spoke against Terry's skin. "This is fucking perfect." After placing a light kiss on the back of his hand, he held it to his chest, keeping Terry's trapped. "I have you in my arms and in my spot. Fucking perfect," he repeated, sounding as if he meant every word.

* * * * *

A sick feeling of dread sat heavy in Brian's gut. He'd spent the day watching Terry slowly decline. Even though his attitude never wavered, the circles under Terry's eyes darkened a little more every time Brian glanced his way. By the time they were driving home from the airport, he'd been so on edge he felt sure he'd snap at any moment. He was positive Terry didn't realize how slow his speech had become before reaching the house. Brian had gratefully grabbed hold of Terry's argument over money to cover how fucking terrified he was. He didn't give a shit about the will. Terry trusted him to take care of things and he would. However, he did care about the way the man moved as if every step he took was through quicksand. Terry had never shown a true moment of fear or weakness in front of Brian before that morning. He would not fail him now that he needed Brian to be the strong one. One half of his body had fallen asleep several minutes earlier. He didn't care. Some part of him believed if he held Terry tight enough, he'd be able to hold him to this world, despite the rattle coming from Terry's chest with every breath he took.

Terry muttered something in his sleep. Brian tilted his chin bringing the man's face into focus. He was pale with the exception of the black rings around each eye and the dark flush across his cheekbones. Brian touched the backs of his fingers to Terry's face. His skin was on fire. The sound of voices and keys jingling caught Brian's attention as Kip came through the door. Cameron was close on her heels still wearing his uniform and carrying ice cream. They both froze when they spotted him. Their identical looks of horror made him wonder what they saw in his expression.

"Brian."

His name fell from Terry's lips in a weak gasp, drawing his worried focus back to his face. Time seemed to slow as Brian met Terry's bright gaze. He opened his mouth as if to say something only a deep rattled breath escaped. He didn't take another. Brian exploded from the couch, dragging Terry with him. Kicking the coffee table aside, he pulled him to the floor.

"Call 911!" His panicked demand was pointless. Cameron already had his phone to his ear. "God damn you, Terry. You promised," he yelled as he checked for a pulse, knowing what he would find. There wasn't one. His chest wasn't moving at all. Brian began CPR without a single thought. The classes Drew had required his employees take came back to him, saving his ass in a moment of desperation. There was a flurry of activity going on around him but Brian didn't see any of it. He had no concept of the passage of time. Even as a paramedic nudged him aside, taking over, Brian couldn't focus on anything except willing Terry to live.

"I have a faint heartbeat."

A roar began in Brian's ears as blood came rushing back to his brain at the words. "Let's get him loaded up."

Brian stood when the paramedics did, keeping pace with them and refusing to leave his side. No one questioned his presence even though he was vaguely aware of Cameron's smoothing the way by explaining he was the spouse. If he spoke to anyone, if they said anything to him, he didn't remember it happening. Nothing felt real.

Hours later, Brian glanced down, surprised to find himself wearing a set of blue scrubs. A mask covered his mouth and nose. Damned if he couldn't remember much of anything from the moment he'd watch Terry take his final breath.

As the last waves of shock fell away, Brian was forced to lock his back teeth together to stop their chatter. Several IV bags hung from a metal pole and three monitors beeped in succession, keeping time with Terry's vitals. A mound of blankets hid his body from view while an oxygen mask covered the lower half of his face. He hadn't regained consciousness. Brian knew because his eyes hadn't left his face.

Now that he seemed to have a working brain cell, Brian took note of their surroundings. He couldn't remember ever seeing this part of the hospital and he'd seen a good deal of it during his mother's final days. This room was different. It was cold and dark. A glass window in the door revealed a second door on the other side, with a small walkway between the two. Moving over to it, Brian glanced down at his feet when his steps felt awkward. Those blue foot things covered his shoes. He didn't know what they were called even though he was sure they had a name. The only time he could remember seeing them was when the AC guy had stopped by to work on his heat and air unit. He slipped them over his shoes to keep from tracking dirt on Brian's carpet.

As Brian stared down at his covered feet, he experienced an odd disconnection from reality. He should've been able to remember putting something so ridiculous over his shoes. As a matter of fact, he should be able to remember putting on his shoes. There was nothing but a blank spot and choking fear. A noise came from the other side of the door bringing his head up. The doctor stood on the other side of the door. As Brian watched, he pulled baggy scrubs over the set he was wearing before covering his hair and feet and pulling on a mask. After washing his hands at the small sink inside the walkway, he pulled on gloves. With his body completely covered, the doctor finally slipped quietly into the room.

"Mr. Richards, I'm Dr. Williams." He held out his hand for Brian to shake and it took him a moment to realize he'd been speaking to him. Adjusting to a new name would take time. He accepted the man's hand.

"You can call me Brian," he said out of habit.

"Fair enough, Brian, since we'll be seeing a lot of one another for the next eight weeks."

"Eight weeks," Brian repeated, unsure of why he'd done so. It seemed the easiest way to keep up his end of the conversation with only a quarter of his mind functioning. The man nodded.

"Your husband has to be the luckiest man on the planet. Not only did you do everything right, we received the all clear from the FDA to administer the medicine needed to get him on the path to recovery."

"I don't understand what happened." Brian didn't know where the confession came from, but there it was. Terry had gone from seemingly fine in the morning to here by the evening.

The doctor nodded again. Even with half his face covered, he could see the sympathy in the man's expression. "Your sister-in-law tells me you were out of town on business during his last stay with us. She went on to add how stubborn Terry is, which I knew, but I didn't realize he wouldn't share my instructions. He was supposed to be on bed rest." Brian knew the muscle in his jaw was ticking but he couldn't make it stop. Dr. Williams hit it dead on. Terry had said no such thing. "Mrs. Travis tells me he took a plane ride instead."

"He did," Brian agreed, hearing the anger in his own voice.

The doctor shook his head. "The air on planes is nasty stuff, full of germs. Terry's system can't take it. My guess is he picked up the virus there. Without any real immune system to fight it, the virus attacked his heart, stopping it. While I don't think there's been any permanent damage, let's fight one battle at a time."

The knowledge Terry had almost died to marry him sat heavy on Brian's chest, suffocating him until he couldn't speak. Luckily, Dr. Williams didn't appear to need any contribution from Brian to keep up the conversation. He ran down the rules of isolation, explaining their dress and the procedure for leaving and entering the room. It turned out he would indeed being seeing a lot of the doctor since it was dangerous for him to come and go. It was safer for Brian to simply stay for the sake of keeping the zone germ free. They made arrangements for McKenna to gather some things to make their long stay more tolerable. Brian had no idea the entire stem cell transplant, chemo, and cell regrowth took so much time. With every word the doctor said, the tightness eased in Brian's chest. There was a plan and a plan meant hope. He would cling to it.

"Brian."

At his name, Brian whipped around in Terry's direction. His eyes were closed and Brian might've thought he was only hearing what he wanted if it weren't for Dr. Williams. Tugging off his stethoscope, he moved to Terry's side.

"Hello again Mr. Richards. We're seeing too much of each other."

Terry's brow furrowed. Brian caught a quick glimpse of light-green irises before his lids fell closed again.

"Brian."

When Terry said his name a second time, he wasted no time taking up his post at his side. Pulling the chair as close to the bed as possible, he dug around beneath the blankets until he found Terry's hand and squeezed it. At the touch, Terry's frown cleared. As the doctor listened to Terry's heart on the opposite side of the bed, Brian did his best to quietly reassure him.

"Everything sounds good. Your heart is beating strong and steady now."

"Has to," Terry whispered. "Doesn't belong to me."

Dr. Williams shook his head as if Terry's words didn't make sense. "He's likely to be disoriented for a few more days." Brian nodded even though he knew exactly what Terry had been trying to say. "I'll let the two of you have some peace. I'll be back to check on you again in a little while and we'll go over the timeline for his treatment." Brian was nodding so much he felt like a bobblehead but he just wanted the man to go away. He was on the verge of losing his shit and the last thing he needed was a witness. After a few more reassuring words, he finally left them alone. The sensation of Terry's thumb brushing over Brian's knuckles ended up being his undoing. Silent tears ran down his face unchecked. The instant Terry had stopped breathing Brian had caught a glimpse of an ugly, bleak future. His whole life, he'd been told people didn't know how much they could endure until they had no other choice. He'd seen a future without Terry and it was more than he could endure. A world without Terry was a world without beauty.

"Chest hurts."

Brian swiped his face across his shoulder. "I had to do CPR. Shit. I hope I didn't crack a rib or anything. I can't even remember if they said."

Terry shook his head. "Your tears hurt my chest."

He swiped at his face again. "No

301

worries. There's nothing but rainbows and happy shit going on over here."

Terry's eyes crinkled in the corners. "Liar."

The knowledge Terry was smiling gave Brian strength. "The hell you say. I've got you and these awesome blue scrubs. I'll have you know, blue happens to be my color." Brian was raring up to be really obnoxious if that's what it took to keep Terry's smiling, but Terry cut him off.

"Love you."

Another tear slipped past his lashes without his permission. "Damn, Terry, I love you too. Don't you ever, ever do that shit to me again."

"I'm not gonna leave you."

With Terry's promise hanging between them, Brian stared hard at the man he loved and had almost lost. He was scared to look away for fear he'd disappear. Terry's eyes opened and he held Brian's gaze. Even with his face mostly covered, Brian knew he was smirking. It set his heart at ease in a way nothing else could.

"Blue isn't your color."

Doing his best to hold back his smile, Brian pulled a hurt face. "I'm wounded. I look hot as hell in these scrubs."

Terry winked. "I'm what looks best on you."

"Ten times better than Armani," Brian agreed, giving into his smile. Sixty years from now, he might have to face his worst fears again. Until then, Terry wasn't going anywhere because he'd given his word he wouldn't and he always got his way.

Chapter Eleven

Eight months later

Jade's fat little cherub cheek looked squished against Terry's muscular shoulder. Her tiny mouth hung open and her soft snores filled the room. Since Terry looked half-asleep as well, he wasn't complaining about the baby sleeping on his shoulder.

"I think she's a bit hopelessly in love with you," Kip said from the living room doorway, mimicking Brian's thoughts. Terry's mouth turned up in one corner. It was an expression that never failed to make Brian's heart skip a beat.

"The feeling is mutual," he murmured quietly in an obvious attempt at not disturbing Kip's daughter. It had taken forever to get her calmed down since losing her favorite pacifier earlier in the day. Even though Jade had—inexplicably—turned out as a blond-haired, blue-eyed angel, she had her mother's fiery redhead attitude and she ruled their home. She took a shuddering breath. Everyone froze. When she didn't stir, Terry stood.

"I'll put her to bed."

Brian's eyes followed him from the room. Kip's low laugh caught his attention as Terry slipped from sight. He smiled, without an ounce of shame. "Hey. He's mine. I can stare if I want."

Kip held her hands up. "I wasn't judging."

"Hmm," he said noncommittally. "What was that laugh then?"

She shook her head. "I was just thinking Jade isn't the only one around here who's a lovesick fool over Terry."

Terry rounded the corner just in

time to catch her final words. "Of course, he is. I'm all things magnificent." Terry crawled onto the couch at Brian's side. Rolling around like a gigantic dog until he was settled with his head in Brian's lap, he added, "It helps that I spoil him rotten." Since Brian couldn't deny it, he decided to let it slide.

"Oh, Jeez. You two are a bit sickening to be around, you know. All your love is choking me so I'll leave you alone to do whatever while I hide in my room and cry about how nobody will ever have me."

"You do that," Terry said, making Brian laugh. They were both used to Kip's fake forever-alone speeches. She didn't mean it. Honestly, Brian knew it was just her way of giving them their space. He appreciated it, especially tonight. He was over-the-moon and bursting with energy. They'd finally gotten the news they'd been waiting on for eight long months. Terry was officially cancer free. Cancer free. Those two words were the most beautiful words in the English language, like music to Brian's ears.

"Goodnight, guys," she called over her shoulder, making her escape when Terry began taunting her by gnawing on the hem of Brian's t-shirt.

"Goodnight, Kip," they answered in unison, managing to sound completely innocent. Another tug at the front of his shirt drew Brian's attention back to his lap. Terry was back to nipping at the material. Brian shook his head at his antics.

"You're in a good mood."

"Ah," Terry said, raising one eyebrow. "Well. I'm about to teach you a new lesson." Inching up the hem, Terry pulled the button loose on Brian's jeans.

He went hard. It was as easy as that. All it took was the insinuation of sexual satisfaction when it came to Terry, and Brian was ready. "In a minute," Terry added, tugging Brian's zipper down. Brian couldn't remember what they were talking about.

"Yeah. In a minute," he agreed, hoping it was the right answer. A knowing smile touched Terry's lips as he set Brian's erection free but he didn't call him on it.

"Damn," Terry breathed, brushing his fingertip across Brian's slit. Everything from the waist down tightened in response to Terry's touch. He kept his gaze locked on the man's every move, hoping not to miss a thing. "I've been thinking about this all day long, craving your salt."

Terry knew how to use his tongue in every way. The words caused an image of Terry on his knees to flash across Brian's mind. His cock leaked and Terry leaned in, capturing the drops with his tongue before closing his lips around Brian's crown. It was so hot inside Terry's mouth. Brian's hips lifted on their own accord, attempting to get deeper. When Terry's cheeks hollowed, Brian found himself reaching for his hair, thankful it had grown back enough to grip. He tugged him closer. Terry obeyed, taking him to the back of his throat. Brian moaned and Terry did it again. This time, he took him deeper. His throat tightened around him. His balls drew up tight as his dick slid across the roof of Terry's mouth. Shifting positions, Terry braced his weight on the palms against the arm of the couch and allowed Brian to set the pace. Brian strained against him. He sucked in a deep breath as the pressure built to a boiling point. It was right there, pressing against the tip of his dick and demanding release. Terry pulled away and went back to resting his head against Brian's thigh as if he didn't intend to move again for the rest of the night.

"We have something to discuss."

Brian's eye twitched at Terry's bright tone. He was hanging onto his sanity by a thread. His body screamed for the blinding orgasm Terry's mouth had promised while his mind struggled to accept Terry didn't intend to finish him off.

"Holy shit, Terry. Are you kidding me?"

Terry's smile hitched up a notch at Brian's frustrated growl. The moisture on his bottom lip teased Brian as he stared at the man's mouth. His cock throbbed.

"It's time for you to challenge Rhys for the title. I know you've only been back to local matches for a couple of months, but you need do this. If you don't, you'll regret it."

"Are we seriously going to talk about this right now?"

Terry wrapped his fingers around Brian's dick and brushed his thumb over the crown. The muscles in Brian's stomach clenched as his nerve endings danced. "Yes. We are. The sooner you give me your word you'll issue the challenge, the sooner I can get back to doing other things with my mouth." He winked, adding fuel the fire.

Brian stared at Terry, shocked. The man was seriously blackmailing him. That cinched it. His husband was fucking evil. Emphasizing his point, Terry squeezed him lightly, tugging upward before letting go. He eyed Brian's erection with open hunger. There was a small part of Brian's brain that recognized he could hold out.

This torture could run both ways, but it was a very small part. Not to mention, Brian didn't want to risk it and he would give Terry anything he wanted.

"Fine. Whatever. I'll talk to Rhys tomorrow."

Terry met his gaze. Satisfaction etched his every line as he took Brian's erection in hand once more. "That wasn't your word."

"Fuck!" Brian roared. "I promise, okay?"

A triumphant mile stretched Terry's lips. "Lesson whatever-number-we're-on-now—if your opponent refuses to submit, make them pay."

The End

Keep an eye out for the next No Rival book, Undamaged.

Author Bio

Charity Parkerson is an award winning and multi-published author with several companies. Born with no filter from her brain to her mouth, she decided to take this odd quirk and insert it in her characters.

*2015 Readers' Favorite Award Winner

*Winner of 2, 2014 Readers' Favorite Awards

*2015 Passionate Plume Award Finalist

*2013 Readers' Favorite Award Winner

*2013 Reviewers' Choice Award Winner

*2012 ARRA Finalist for Favorite Paranormal Romance

*Five-time winner of The Mistress of the Darkpath

Connect with her online:

--Website: charityparkerson.com

--Facebook:

facebook.com/authorCharityParkerson

facebook.com/TheMenofSin

--Twitter: twitter.com/CharityParkerso

www.ingramcontent.com/pod-product-compliance
Lightning Source LLC
Chambersburg PA
CBHW050700290626
47170CB00016B/2529